SECRET LOVE

Through the open door Robbie could see the lamp which stood by his bed, and it must have been lit before Josofine went out and although it was turned low the room seemed warm and golden.

Josofine moved to the window to look down at the moonlit street below.

"It has been a lovely evening," she sighed. "I do not think I have ever been so happy."

"Nor have I," Robbie replied.

"Is that true?" she quizzed.

"Of course it is true. Surely you understand that when I am with you I am happier than I have ever been."

Josephine looked at him and he realised that her blue eyes were searching his face – she wanted to be quite sure he was telling her the truth.

Very slowly, as if he was afraid to do so, he put his arms round her.

"I love you, Josofine," he whispered. "I love you, my darling, with all my heart and soul. There is no one else in the whole world for me except you."

He felt the little quiver that went through her and then he drew her closer to him and his lips were on hers.

It was a very gentle kiss.

A kiss almost of reverence.

THE BARBARA CARTLAND
PINK COLLECTION

Titles in this series

SECRET LOVE

BARBARA CARTLAND

Barbaracartland.com Ltd

THE BARBARA CARTLAND PINK COLLECTION

Dame Barbara Cartland is still regarded as the most prolific bestselling author in the history of the world.

In her lifetime she was frequently in the Guinness Book of Records for writing more books than any other living author.

Her most amazing literary feat was to double her output from 10 books a year to over 20 books a year when she was 77 to meet the huge demand.

She went on writing continuously at this rate for 20 years and wrote her very last book at the age of 97, thus completing an incredible 400 books between the ages of 77 and 97.

Her publishers finally could not keep up with this phenomenal output, so at her death in 2000 she left behind an amazing 160 unpublished manuscripts, something that no other author has ever achieved.

Barbara's son, Ian McCorquodale, together with his daughter Iona, felt that it was their sacred duty to publish all these titles for Barbara's millions of admirers all over the world who so love her wonderful romances.

So in 2004 they started publishing the 160 brand new Barbara Cartlands as *The Barbara Cartland Pink Collection*, as Barbara's favourite colour was always pink – and yet more pink!

The Barbara Cartland Pink Collection is published monthly exclusively by Barbaracartland.com and the books are numbered in sequence from 1 to 160.

Enjoy receiving a brand new Barbara Cartland book each month by taking out an annual subscription to the Pink Collection, or purchase the books individually.

The Pink Collection is available from the Barbara Cartland website www.barbaracartland.com via mail order and through all good bookshops.

In addition Ian and Iona are proud to announce that The Barbara Cartland Pink Collection is now available in ebook format as from Valentine's Day 2011.

For more information, please contact us at:

Barbaracartland.com Ltd.
Camfield Place
Hatfield
Hertfordshire AL9 6JE
United Kingdom

Telephone: +44 (0)1707 642629
Fax: +44 (0)1707 663041
Email: info@barbaracartland.com

THE LATE DAME BARBARA CARTLAND

Barbara Cartland who sadly died in May 2000 at the age of nearly 99 was the world's most famous romantic novelist who wrote 723 books in her lifetime with worldwide sales of over 1 billion copies and her books were translated into 36 different languages.

As well as romantic novels, she wrote historical biographies, 6 autobiographies, theatrical plays, books of advice on life, love, vitamins and cookery. She also found time to be a political speaker and television and radio personality.

She wrote her first book at the age of 21 and this was called *Jigsaw*. It became an immediate bestseller and sold 100,000 copies in hardback and was translated into 6 different languages. She wrote continuously throughout her life, writing bestsellers for an astonishing 76 years. Her books have always been immensely popular in the United States, where in 1976 her current books were at numbers 1 & 2 in the B. Dalton bestsellers list, a feat never achieved before or since by any author.

Barbara Cartland became a legend in her own lifetime and will be best remembered for her wonderful romantic novels, so loved by her millions of readers throughout the world.

Her books will always be treasured for their moral message, her pure and innocent heroines, her good looking and dashing heroes and above all her belief that the power of love is more important than anything else in everyone's life.

"Love, I have always believed, is a gift from God and, as you respect and revere God, you must respect and revere love – or else it can melt away and return to God."

Barbara Cartland

CHAPTER ONE
1868

Wenda walked down from the stables towards the house.

She had been out riding early and was now thinking about all that was waiting for her inside.

She had realised long ago that it was impossible to make the house look as it had in her parents' day.

She could only do her very best to make part of it habitable and comfitable for her brother and herself.

Unfortunately for Wenda, Robert or Robbie as they always called him, had found a year ago that he preferred London to the country.

As they could not afford everything he desired, she could understand it. He enjoyed the parties that took place every night in Mayfair and were obviously far more entertaining than the routine of life at Creswell Court.

She saw Robbie intermittently, but it was almost five weeks since she had last heard from him and she could only hope that he would be home soon.

There was so much she needed to discuss with him and so much they must decide if the estate was not to go completely to rack and ruin.

As it was there were endless repairs that had been neglected simply because, as Wenda knew, they could not afford to pay for them.

Her father, Lord Creswell, had been an extremely brilliant man.

Queen Victoria had found him of great assistance to her especially after she became a widow, but unfortunately that did not provide enough money for him to keep up the estate that had been in the Creswell family for centuries.

All through history land had played a significant part in ensuring the strength and well-being of England and with her parents both dead and her brother still young and unmarried, Wenda felt sadly that no one was particularly interested in The Court itself.

At one time it had been one of the great sights of Britain and it was close to London and thus easy to reach.

There had always been, when her father was alive, people coming to stay for a few days or even driving down just to see the beauty of The Court and all it contained.

Each successive 'Lord of the Manor', as her father was often called, had contributed to its notable collection of pictures, which had been started during the reign of Henry VIII and added to by every succeeding generation.

It was a Creswell who had helped James I to bring in the Entailment Act and this had preserved the collection from being severely depleted in the time of George IV.

Lord Creswell and his friends, such as the Earl of Coventry and other Peers, were throwing away their finest possessions at the gambling tables.

The Earl of Coventry had lost Coventry Street in London on one turn of the cards and many other Peers had lost their property in the same way.

When her father was hard-up, he had often said to Wenda,

"It's a very good thing I cannot sell anything from the house. Otherwise my son would indeed have just cause to reproach me and so I imagine would you."

"It would be awful, Papa, if we did not have the beautiful pictures to look at, and of course the silver which, as you have often told me, is unique."

"The finest silver in England became ours at the time of George III," stated Lord Creswell. "But I am quite certain it would have been dissipated by our ancestor who was notorious for making higher bets at White's and other Clubs than anyone had ever done before!"

Wenda sighed.

"We could certainly do with that money now, Papa, especially as we need new horses."

"The one thing I refuse to economise on," he had replied, "is our horses. It is the only pleasure left to me and I intend to ride the best bred and the fastest until I am in the grave."

Wenda had laughed, but he had indulged his wish, unfortunately leaving behind him debts and extravagant commitments that she and Robbie had attempted to meet during the last five years.

And they had not, Wenda thought with a sigh, been particularly successful.

She had now almost reached the front of the house and to her surprise she saw there was a man waiting by the steps leading up to the front door.

As she drew nearer she saw it was Donson, one of the younger men who worked on the land and also when required in the stables.

She thought from the expression on his face before she reached him that he had bad news to tell her and she wondered what could have occurred to upset him.

"Good morning, Donson," she greeted him. "Are you waiting for me?"

"I am, Miss Wenda," he replied.

She did not need to ask him if there was anything wrong.

"I've been told," he began, "because I were late this mornin', I be not needed no longer."

Wenda gave a little cry.

"Oh, Donson! Who said that?"

She knew the answer even before she even asked.

It was Hatton the Factor, who was in charge of the land and was a rather difficult man to work with. He drove those under him hard and there was no doubt that he got more out of the land than anyone else would have done.

"Yon Mr. Hatton's been at I for some time, Miss Wenda," Donson answered. "And there be nothin' I does that pleases 'im, you can be sure of that."

"He has really told you, Donson, not to come back tomorrow?"

Donson nodded vigorously.

He was a nice looking man nearing twenty-five and on the whole a good worker, but Wenda, who called at all the cottages in the village, was aware he had difficulties at home.

Donson's father was dead, his sisters were married and there was only he and a younger brother who was still at school to look after their mother, a helpless invalid who could not walk by herself and yet somehow she managed to cook their meals for them.

Wenda felt especially sorry for the boys as it meant, before they went to work or school, they had to help their mother dress and then place her into a chair so she could propel herself about the cottage.

"I've been a little late two or three times recently," Donson was saying, "because me mother, as you knows, Miss Wenda, can't dress 'erself and 'er be real poorly in the mornin's and finds it hard to get out of bed."

4

"Did you explain to Mr. Hatton that was why you were late this morning?"

"I tells 'im as I tells 'im before, but 'e won't listen to me and be pleased of an excuse for me to go. And you knows as well as I does, Miss Wenda, that the cottage goes with the job and I've nowhere else to take Mother."

Wenda knew that this was the truth.

At the same time she felt that pleading with Hatton would not be of any use. He had always disliked Donson who undoubtedly had a way of answering him back and he would have been pleased to find an excuse to be rid of him.

However she felt, if only for his mother's sake, she must do something to help the family.

The main difficulty was always the same – *money*.

It was hard enough to get Robbie to give her money for the food they ate at The Court when he was away and Wenda was sure it would be quite hopeless to ask him for more than he was providing already.

The only possession of her own was the jewellery that had belonged to her mother and she had thought when her mother died she would never sell it.

In fact she had firmly resisted various suggestions tentatively made by her brother that she should sell some of the jewels. Even so they were not much use to her and with the proceeds they could undoubtedly employ more people on the estate and in the house.

Wenda had consistently refused, but she knew now that the precious jewels would have to be sold if she was to help Donson.

"I understand, Donson," she said quietly, "that you do not get on with Mr. Hatton, and of course I cannot go against his decision not to employ you on the estate."

She saw his expression before she went on quickly,

"I shall employ you myself to work in the garden. Things have been too much for me lately and it always looked so beautiful when I was a child."

"You means that, Miss Wenda, you'll take I on as a gardener? You knows I'll do my best for you and it'll be a real joy to be away from that Mr. Hatton. He 'ates I and there be nothin' I can do to please 'im."

"Well you will have to work very hard to please *me*, Donson. You know as well as I do that the garden is in a real mess this spring and needs so much doing to it."

"You leave it to I, Miss Wenda, and I'll not let you down."

Donson took a deep breath and added,

"I be real thankful, I be. It'd break Mother's 'eart if her 'ad to go to the workhouse."

"I know it would and you will stay in your cottage even though you will not be working on the estate. I will arrange it with Mr. Hatton and with his Lordship."

"Well, all I can say, Miss Wenda, is that I thanks you, as I know me mother'll thank you, from the bottom of her 'eart, and I'll make that garden of yours a sight for sore eyes, that I promise you."

Wenda smiled at him.

"You can start right away. You will find my tools inside the toolshed, but be careful to put them back every evening and whatever you do, don't break them."

"I'll take real care of 'em, I promise you that."

Donson went off joyfully in a way that she knew had always annoyed Mr. Hatton as it told the world that he was pleased with life.

He had the type of temper which was very much up or down and she could imagine all too clearly what he must have felt when Mr. Hatton dismissed him.

She had often thought he was difficult, but he got more out of the estate than anyone else could. They had so few men and so many acres requiring attention.

Wenda went into the house and straight upstairs to her bedroom.

She opened the drawer where she kept her mother's jewellery.

She seldom if ever had a chance to wear it, but she often looked at it and fondled it as it made her remember how beautiful her mother had looked when she went out to dinner with her father or attended a local Hunt Ball.

She could quite understand when she was told how her mother had been acknowledged as one of the most beautiful women in Society.

As soon as her father had seen her, he had fallen head over heels in love with her.

The daughter of the Duke of Netherton, she had been expected to make a distinguished marriage and then to everyone's great surprise she had married Lord Creswell with his fine family tree but very little money.

There was little doubt that because he was just so handsome and so charming nothing mattered to either of them except to be together.

As the years passed they became poorer and poorer, but it never troubled them.

They laughed whenever things went right and when things went wrong and they were blissfully happy not only with themselves but with their two children.

There was little doubt that Robbie was as good-looking and as intelligent as his father and Wenda was an adorable beautiful baby looking like a small round angel.

She grew up as the years passed to look more and more like her mother.

Unfortunately by the time Wenda should have burst upon London Society, her father was dead and her mother died very shortly afterwards.

Wenda had always believed that it was impossible for them to be apart and she was sure that when they were dead they would find each other again.

Her father had caught a virulent disease at the time when he was inspecting foreign ships entering the Port of London from the East at the request of the Government.

There had been stories of drugs smuggled ashore for large sums of money as well as other articles banned by Parliament and it was in China Town in the East End of London that Lord Creswell had inspected a ship from China and discovered a large amount of drugs and untested foods.

To prove to himself they were right in arresting the Captain of the ship he had tasted the foods himself and in doing so contracted an Eastern disease for which there was no cure.

He died in a few days, leaving his wife prostrate with grief.

Five months later Wenda had found her mother dead in bed when she called her at eight in the morning. She thought at first that she was sleeping as she looked so happy with a smile on her beautiful lips.

And it seemed impossible that she would not open her large eyes and laugh as she always had.

It was fortunate that Robbie was at home rather than in London as he so often was since leaving Oxford and he had taken over everything including the running of the estate and Creswell Court.

Although Wenda was six years younger than him, she managed to help him in many ways that no one else would have been able to do.

It was together they discovered how many debts there were.

Their father had happily enjoyed life with the wife he loved and he had actually spent as little time as possible at Windsor Castle at the beck and call of the Queen.

Her Majesty had sent her deepest condolences and was obviously upset at the news of their father's death, but that did not help them to pay his huge debts.

It was only by selling everything that was saleable with the exception of the family jewels that now belonged to Wenda, that Robbie managed to put the house and the estate more or less in order.

He had been here, there and everywhere – from the time he rose in the morning until nightfall.

It was only in the last year when he had gone to London that Wenda realised how much depended on him.

Now missing him desperately she tried to make the house look as beautiful as it had always been and to be a happy place for him when he did come home.

'If only we had a little more money,' she sighed as she looked in the drawer at her mother's jewellery.

The collection consisted of gifts at different times from the husband who loved her.

There was a brooch her mother had received from her parents as a wedding present and because there was no sentiment attached to it, Wenda was now prepared to sell it rather than the beautiful pieces her father had given her mother as a sign of his love on her birthdays.

Wenda thought that as the diamonds in the brooch were fairly large and a good colour, she should therefore obtain a good price for it.

In which case she could not only pay Donson's wages, but would perhaps be able to afford someone extra in the house.

It was impossible for Banks, the old butler, who had been with the family for over thirty years and his wife who was the cook to manage the house as well.

So Wenda employed two women who came in from the village and they cleaned the part of the house Wenda and Robbie used.

But there were a great number of rooms which were closed and remained untended, unless Wenda herself saw to them and as she could not bear things not to be exactly as her mother had wanted them, she spent a great deal of time brushing, dusting and washing.

And this included the large number of pictures that were really valuable and the silver which filled the pantry safe.

Just a few items which they used when Robbie was at home were kept shining by Banks, while all the George III collection stayed at the back of the safe covered with green baize to protect it from tarnish.

'I will go to St. Albans tomorrow,' thought Wenda, taking the diamond brooch from the drawer, 'and see what the jeweller there will offer me.'

Then she thought it was a silly thing to do – surely it would fetch more in London.

Therefore she should wait until Robbie came home and seek his advice and in the meantime she would have to overdraw a bit more from the bank to pay Donson's wages.

Slowly she put the diamond brooch back into its case and then as she looked at the other cases, she could not help wondering how soon they too would have to go.

'Surely there must be something else to sell,' she told herself.

But she knew it was a stupid remark.

Her father had sold everything he said was saleable when they began to be hard-up.

A list of everything that was entailed lay on the desk in the library and Wenda knew her father had sat up late night after night going through it to see if something saleable had been overlooked.

Three Trustees had been appointed to inspect the house at various intervals and they would, she was quite certain, not miss one object on the long list.

She closed the drawer of the dressing table.

The best thing she could do would be to write to Robbie to tell him he must come home as soon as possible.

She had something special to ask of him, but she thought he would not be too pleased at being called back.

Yet she knew it would be a mistake to make their overdraft at the bank any bigger than it was already – the Bank Manager had in fact been very kind in allowing them to overdraw as much as they had.

"I well know the difficulties you are up against, my Lord," he said the last time Robbie saw him. "And I will do my best to help you, but you know as well as I do it is a great mistake to run up large debts you cannot repay. It is something your father always tried not to do."

Robbie knew this was true, though he had not been very successful, but then his father had had things to sell.

He had also been lucky for several successive years in having excellent harvests and these had paid for all the expenditure on the estate.

Last year's harvest however had been a bad one and although there were hopes that this year's would be better, they were considerably short of labourers on the estate.

'I *must* get in touch with Robbie,' Wenda thought as she went down the stairs.

Then to her surprise she heard the sound of wheels and horses moving in the courtyard and she wondered who it could possibly be so early in the morning.

If they were neighbours coming to call, they usually came at teatime as was correct and she was not expecting anyone wanting to see her until after breakfast.

As she heard the carriage draw up outside the front door, she then hurried downstairs as Banks would be in the kitchen and not dressed correctly to receive a visitor.

Then before she could reach the door it opened and as she descended the last of the stairs, she gave a cry of astonishment and delight.

"*Robbie*! Robbie! I was just thinking of you."

Her brother came into the hall and taking off his hat tossed it down on a chair.

"Why have you come home so early? And how is it possible you are here just when I need you?"

The words seemed to tumble out of Wenda's lips.

Her brother kissed her as he said calmly,

"One thing at a time. I will tell you what it is all about, but first I am hoping there is breakfast for me."

"Of course there is, Robbie. I will go and tell Mrs. Banks you have arrived and she will be thrilled to see you, as naturally I am."

Her brother did not answer her and she noticed him looking up in what she thought was a strange manner at the pictures in the hall.

Then she hurried along the passage to the kitchen to find Mrs. Banks cooking her breakfast and Banks in his shirtsleeves laying the tray to carry into the breakfast room.

"Who do you think has arrived?" Wenda asked as she opened the door. "His Lordship!"

"His Lordship!" Banks exclaimed. "*At this hour*!"

"Yes, and I was just thinking how much I wanted to see him. But he is here and needless to say, Mrs. Banks, he is hungry."

"If he's come all that way from London this early, then the poor young gentleman'll be nothin' else, but he'll have to wait a moment while I cooks some more eggs and bacon for him or you can start him off, Miss Wenda, with what I've cooked for you."

"That is a good idea. Bring it in, Banks, as soon as it is ready and I will wait for the second serving if I can get to it before Robbie eats that too!"

She laughed and the servants who loved them both were laughing with her.

She went back into the breakfast room and found Robbie, to her surprise, holding a silver dish in his hand. It was always filled with fruit when in season, but otherwise remained as an ornament on the sideboard.

"It's so wonderful to see you," sighed Wenda. "It really was strange that I was just praying that I could be in touch with you and tell you I needed your help."

"And I want yours, Wenda, but I was brought up to say 'ladies first', so *you* tell me what your trouble is."

"As you can guess, it's to do with money."

Robbie groaned almost theatrically,

"How could I think it could be anything else?"

"I will tell you what has happened, Robbie."

She sat down putting her elbows on the table and resting her chin on her hands.

"You may be angry with me," she began, "but I am sure what I did was right."

She told him as quickly as she could, so as not to bore him, how she had met Donson when she was coming back from the stables and how he had told her that Hatton had sacked him.

Robbie did not speak so she continued that it would be impossible for the two boys to find another cottage for their disabled mother.

13

Wenda was breathless as she finished and waited apprehensively for Robbie to reply.

"Of course you were right to keep him, Wenda."

She gave a little cry.

"Oh, Robbie, I was hoping you would say that. But I was so worried you would be cross with me."

"How could I say anything else? Papa would have turned in his grave if we had turned out Mrs. Donson with nowhere to go except the workhouse. I am told conditions are harsh there and the inmates are fed abominably."

"I heard that too," said Wenda. "Papa did not make a fuss about it in case they asked him for more money than he had given them already.

There was silence and after a moment she added,

"You were unable to give them anything yourself last year, so I doubt if you complained they would listen."

"We are not going to send anyone to the workhouse if I can help it. At the same time I must have some money, Wenda, and at once."

Wenda gave another cry.

"Oh, Robbie, how can you ask for money like that? Unless it's a very small sum. I will pay Donson myself when I sell this brooch."

"What brooch, Wenda?"

"It is a brooch of Mama's and I have been looking at it upstairs. I don't want to sell any of Mama's jewellery. It is absolutely all, as you know, that I possess. But if I am to pay Donson, I want you to sell the brooch for as much as you possibly can."

She saw he was listening and added quickly,

"Of course what we get for it will have to be kept for his wages week after week.

14

"I have another idea," Robbie answered.

"I have not even asked you why you have arrived so early and unexpectedly. What has happened in London? You are not in trouble, Robbie?"

"No, nothing like that – very much the opposite, but what I have to tell you may be a bit of a shock."

Wenda looked at him somewhat uneasily.

"I think I told you that I was so thrilled when a little while ago the Prince of Wales invited me to Marlborough House and I have been there a number of times since."

"Oh, Robbie, how exciting for you! I am longing to hear what Marlborough House is like inside."

"It is very large, very comfortable and very rich!"

Wenda's eyes were shining as he answered.

She worried about him when he was in London and because he was so good-looking he might be taken up by the wrong set that her parents had so disapproved of.

Living quietly in the country she had nevertheless heard about the strange behaviour of some of the younger members of Society which would have surely shocked and disgusted her father and mother.

And now with her elbows still on the table and her small pointed chin resting on her hands, she asked eagerly,

"Tell me, tell me all about it, Robbie, and of course about the Prince of Wales."

"That is just what I am going to do. I expect you know, as I do, what a miserable time he has because he is not permitted by Queen Victoria to take any part in the affairs of the country."

"Yes, Papa used to talk about that and it seems so extraordinary that now he is so much older she still will not let him help her."

Looking back Wenda recalled that her father had often been voluble on how the Prince of Wales had been educated and brought up in the wrong way.

Whenever he was summoned to Windsor Castle, he nearly always returned with some story about the Prince and inevitably it concerned the worry he was to his mother.

What had happened was that Queen Victoria and Prince Albert had decided their son should be an absolute model of Victorian morality and were determined that his education should be different from the way in which their predecessors had been brought up.

The result of this was that the Prince of Wales was guarded by Tutors, lectured by Professors and subjected to long sermons from Bishops.

At Cambridge he was scrutinised, watched over, and cut off from all the other undergraduates, in case they might pollute him into behaving as they did.

Even when he joined the Grenadier Guards, he was not allowed to undertake the duties of an ordinary Officer or mix with his comrades and the other Officers were sorry for him constantly under such close supervision.

One of the young actresses who was taken up by the Grenadiers was a pretty girl called Nelly Clinton and they smuggled her past the General supervising the Prince and into his quarters.

He found her waiting for him as a birthday present when he went to bed!

The future King of England quickly learnt the facts of life and his brother Officers believed they were really doing him a favour. They had no idea of the calamity they were bringing down on his head.

Unfortunately, like many of her successors, Nelly Clinton was only too well aware of the honour conferred on her and as invariably happens in such circumstances, she talked and boasted proudly of her conquest and it was only a question of time before what had happened found its way back to Windsor Castle.

Lord Torrington, a Gentleman-in-Waiting, who was known as a gossip, thought it his duty to inform Prince Albert that his son had been sleeping with an actress and from that moment the Prince's life had become what any other young man would have called 'a complete hell'.

The Prince was made to apologise over and over again to his father and write countless letters of penitence to his mother.

Eventually they had both forgiven him, but Prince Albert had not been well for some time.

After seeing his son he complained of headaches and catarrh and he could not sleep because he had pains in his body.

On the 2nd December 1861 he collapsed and twelve days later died. The cause of his death was typhoid.

But the Queen was convinced that if it had not been for the terrible behaviour of her son, her beloved Albert would not have passed away.

She had absorbed a very rigid idea of morality from her German husband and to her therefore the Prince's small escapade with the pretty actress was not a 'youthful error'.

He had fallen by the wayside and it confirmed her worst fears for the future of the British Monarchy.

Although he had suffered a great deal at the hands of his father, the Prince had definitely been fond of him, but it was cruel and wrong to make out, as the Queen did, that he had committed an unforgivable sin.

But all these constrictions undoubtedly made him determined that one day he would be free, and one day he would be able to enjoy himself in the way he wished to do.

Hearing all about it from her father and listening to hushed conversations about him, Wenda felt very sorry for the Prince.

There had also been a great deal of gossip about him later and Wenda had however heard little of it because her parents never talked about it in front of her.

Living in the country she was unaware of what was happening in London but nevertheless she was exceedingly interested in the Prince and his wife. She was the beautiful Princess Alexandra he had married at twenty-one.

Wenda now waited breathlessly for her brother to tell her what he had been doing.

"I have been most fortunate," Robbie was saying, "in that the Prince of Wales now counts me as one of his friends. I have been to Marlborough House a great deal and I have been included in Royal house parties."

"House parties!" Wenda exclaimed. "Do you mean you stayed with the Prince and Princess at Sandringham?"

"I have not been to Sandringham yet, but I am sure I will be asked."

"That is thrilling for you! I cannot wait for you to tell me all about it."

"What I am really waiting to tell you," said Robbie, "and I am not quite certain what you will feel about it, is that *the Prince of Wales wants to come here*."

Wenda stared at him.

"Come here! You must be joking!"

"No, I mean it – although it is rather difficult to explain why."

"But there must be hundreds of houses for him to visit," protested Wenda.

"Yes, of course there are, but he always wants to go somewhere new where he has not been before and that is why he has asked to come here."

"I don't believe it, Robbie! You must have been dreaming that he invited himself."

"No, he actually has, and I cannot refuse him. He wants to come *this weekend*."

Wenda gasped.

"I think you have gone mad, Robbie!"

CHAPTER TWO

All the way down from London Robbie was trying to work out how he could explain it all to his sister.

He realised that, living in the country and being so young, she knew very little about the Social world. Also little, if anything, about men.

It was thus very difficult to put into words what he was thinking and feeling about the Prince of Wales or how much it meant to him to be one of H.R.H.'s friends.

In previous years there had been an unwritten law that whatever happened or whatever the Prince of Wales did, it was on no account to be known to the newspapers – the parties that he attended which were his joy and delight were to be kept as quiet as possible.

To amuse himself the Prince had to make up for the long empty years of his boyhood when he was guarded and protected from all temptations to immorality.

He had been married off when he was only twenty-one and Queen Victoria believed that only being married would keep him away from dangerous women.

However there were still rumours and scandal in the background and the Prince himself began to realise that he must be extremely careful that nothing he did leaked out into the newspapers.

Unfortunately any scandals concerning his friends reverted on him and he was finding it difficult by the end of the 1860s to keep at bay the greatest enemy of them all – boredom.

His friends and Society as a whole did their best to keep him happy and the Social world made a tremendous fuss of him.

He was not a great wit, but he enjoyed anecdotes and these were collected by everyone he knew to amuse him. When conversation failed it was difficult to find other interests until they discovered that the Heir to the Throne enjoyed a practical joke.

He laughed loudly when shaving-soap was put into the meringues and louder still when Lord Dupplin found a live lobster in his bed.

As Robbie was to learn there was much more to the Prince of Wales than large meals, large cigars and large women.

He had been brought up to rule, but ruling was the one activity he was not allowed to do and he still longed to peep into all the red boxes from which his mother directed British foreign policy, but he could not touch them.

He was therefore forced, whether he wanted to or not, to continue to enjoy himself.

The only difficulty was to find any variation that would take his fancy.

His closest friends did their very best, but they were frightened of the nosey newspapers, which became more dangerous as the years passed.

Then the Prince of Wales's friends decided among themselves that they would make their enjoyment more secretive than it had ever been – but, most important of all, keep what was happening from the Queen.

It was after a scandal that the Prince was involved in, although he had had very little part in it, that the idea of *house parties* was introduced.

They immediately became a success and the Prince of Wales's wealthy friends all loved to be exploited by him.

Husbands whose wives he slept with felt it was an honour and the 'ladies of the town' all spoke of him most tenderly. They all naturally claimed vigorously to have received his favours whether it was true or not.

At Marlborough House he played the host and he made certain that everyone enjoyed themselves.

At Sandringham, wearing his well-cut tweeds, he made the ideal Country Squire. He hunted, shot and spent a great deal of money on the house and the estate.

What was really most important from the Prince's point of view was that Sandringham became the home of Princess Alexandra and their five children and he was the doting father, humane and understanding.

Even the Queen felt they were being kept from contamination by Society at Sandringham.

But the Prince of Wales still required something new and something different.

This came about when he realised that the actresses and 'ladies of the town' in whom he had been interested talked too much and sooner or later what they said reached Windsor Castle.

It was then that the Prince, or one of his favourite friends, started the idea of house parties.

Each guest took with him the lady of his choice and they indulged themselves at a 'secret weekend' and there were no gossips around proclaiming to all and sundry what had happened.

The Prince's closest friends at this particular time were the Duke of Sutherland, Lord John Carrington, Lord Charles Beresford and Lord Hardwicke and they were invariably beside him at every party.

But it was wise for the host if he could introduce someone new to whom His Royal Highness would take a liking and there were certain rules not written down but obeyed by everyone who entertained the Prince.

They must be careful not to invite anyone who had caused a scandal, like the Marquis of Hastings, who had actually been the Prince's earliest guide to the low life of the City – rich and irresistible he had become a dangerous influence on the Prince, as was feared by Queen Victoria.

The Marquis had developed a passion for the seedy side of life and criminals made him feel at home in their brothels and the sailors' dives at Rotherhithe.

He squandered a huge fortune on lunatic bets and slow horses, but he remained a favourite companion of the Prince when he went to any of the lower haunts of London.

At Mott's Dancing Rooms in Folly Street, a very low but undoubtedly amusing place, he was known to be a 'hell-raiser'.

And it was at Mott's that Hastings had perpetrated one of the most outrageous and talked about jokes of the year.

He had paid a rat-catcher twenty guineas to produce two hundred fully grown sewer rats, tied them up in sacks and when the dancing was at its height on the Marquis's instructions one of his friends turned out the lights.

It was then that his Lordship released the rats and pandemonium broke out amongst the female dancers.

The jape made the Marquis's name as one of the liveliest blades in Society, but Her Majesty the Queen was not amused.

The Prince now however was growing older and he enjoyed comfortable weekends in comfortable houses more than the Dance Halls of his rakish youth.

It was not surprising that his friends were only too glad to pander to this new idea, which started the unwritten law that for a husband it was more a duty than dishonour to allow his wife to be the object of the Royal passion.

Naturally the Prince benefitted by this enormously.

He had no taste for young unmarried girls, who had no Social experience and thus never appealed to him, but he did require endless variations and, what was even more dangerous in many ways, plenty of excitement.

He loved women and he had been forbidden them when he was young, so he gloried in his power to attract them – even, it seemed, to make them fall in love with him.

It was not for nothing that he gained the reputation of being 'a great lover'.

The difficulty which always confronted his friends was to give him variety and to keep his *affaires-de-coeur* hidden from the public.

He particularly enjoyed making new friends among the aristocracy, but he was always loyal to those who had been loyal to him.

After being scrupulously guarded, supervised and watched by his mother, he was suddenly free and he found himself not only loved by so many but envied because of his Royal position.

It was just what he had always longed for, but he believed it was impossible for him to have any freedom until he became King.

When he met young Lord Creswell, he had been charming to him and they reminisced over Robbie's father, who had always gone out of his way to help the Prince.

After the first invitations to Marlborough House the Prince had found Robbie to be amusing and witty – a man who enjoyed life almost as much as he enjoyed it himself.

Then Robbie found himself invited almost nightly by the Prince or his friends to make up a party and it was then he learnt about and enjoyed the secret weekends when they stayed in the same large comfortable country houses.

Each gentleman took the lady he was particularly interested in at that moment and there was no need to warn the Prince's special friends that the women they invited must be acceptable in Society.

They needed therefore to arrange the parties so that they did not interfere with the real Lady of the House.

This was usually easy in the same way as Princess Alexandra and her children stayed at Sandringham, most of the Prince's friends would keep their wives and children in the country, especially in the summer when the boys were home from school.

As Robbie reflected when he was driving as fast as possible to Creswell Court, it was in Paris where the Prince had really found his liberation.

He had not thought of telling Wenda when he had gone abroad, but he had accompanied the Prince and found the glittering City something he had never imagined in his wildest dreams.

The *cocottes* and *courtesans* dominated the smart life of Paris making France so different from England ruled over by Queen Victoria.

These exciting and beautiful women were the real celebrities of Paris and many owned their own sumptuous houses with a string of wealthy and titled lovers in tow.

The Prince of Wales was popular in Paris and he and his party of friends were hailed with delight whenever they appeared.

Robbie had been introduced to La Païva, who was a Russian. She was the most expensive and most celebrated *courtesan* of the age and she had just opened her mansion in the *Champs Elysées*.

He also met Cora Pearl, a young English girl from Plymouth who had become the mistress of the Emperor of France and every member of the Jockey Club!

The Prince of Wales had been fascinated by her on a previous visit and it was for him that at the *Café Anglais* she had been served up naked beneath an enormous silver cover as the *piece de resistance*.

Robbie was amazed to find that the Prince of Wales travelled as the Earl of Chester, besides having his own suite at the Hotel Bristol.

If he was to really enjoy Paris, Robbie's enjoyment exceeded his. He had never known that love affairs could be carried on in such a surprising and extravagant way.

He laughed, thinking if he never saw Paris again, it would always remain in his memory as one of the most delicious moments of his life.

There were many other parties for Robbie after they returned to England and it was when he was dining two days ago at Marlborough House that the blow struck.

Princess Alexandra was visiting her family abroad and had not yet returned and it was the Duke of Sutherland who had asked vaguely,

"What are we doing next weekend?"

The others at the table looked at the Prince eagerly as it was always he who had a pertinent suggestion to make and who invariably made any party memorable.

They recalled all the discreetly chosen actresses and the Prince's private secretary, Francis Knollys, arranged it for him at a chosen rendezvous.

But what had been different lately was the married ladies of the Prince's circle, who he seemed to prefer to the glamorous beauties of the stage who were often somewhat disappointing when the footlights were switched off.

It was well known to Robbie and the others present that His Royal Highness usually visited the married ladies he was currently interested in at their own houses in the afternoon.

It was understood that after tea husbands went to their Clubs and the servants to the basement, and another unwritten law was that no one asked questions if a hansom cab bearing the Prince of Wales's crest was seen standing outside a front door in Mayfair or Belgravia.

What was also on the list of amusements and in fact now ranked number one, was the entertainment of beauties who were in Royal favour and who could only be properly enjoyed quietly and secretively in a weekend house party when the Mistress of the house was not present.

This was where Francis Knollys would arrange that the ladies invited had no other engagements that particular weekend.

And there was of course one vital condition to all these arrangements – that was there must never be any scandal or embarrassment for the Prince of Wales.

The Society he controlled allowed him to make the rules and the prime condition of his friendship to those who surrounded him was that he must never suffer damage to his reputation as the future King of England.

It was recognised, when people looked back, as one of the greatest achievements of the Prince's life that he had managed to create an exclusive Social sexual game for the English Society to play without fear.

Naturally it was a game in which he made the rules and enjoyed himself personally with undiminished vigour until he was well past middle age.

But to Robbie it was all new, exciting and different.

At the same time he was only too easily aware that just as he had been picked up and become to all intents and purposes a close friend of the Prince of Wales, he would, if he made a mistake, be just as easily dropped.

He had inherited his father's native intelligence and he appreciated that it was very important for him to keep the Prince's friendship and not, as some of his friends had done, lose it suddenly overnight.

He had therefore just managed not to exclaim with horror when the Prince had proposed,

"I have just thought of one house I have not visited, which I have always heard is very fine and has a superb collection of pictures."

"Where is that?" someone asked.

Robbie froze as the Prince replied,

"Creswell Court. I remember my father telling me how many treasures it contains. Is that not true, Robbie?"

For a moment it was difficult for Robbie to speak and then he replied rather tremulously,

"It is still there, sir, and as you say has an excellent collection of pictures."

"Then that is where we will go next weekend," the Prince declared. "I feel sure your father, Robbie, would like me to see it and I bet you have some excellent horses we can ride."

There was nothing Robbie could say except that it would be a great honour to welcome him.

"Very well," the Prince had said, "as it is quite near it will be far easier to drive there than to have my private coach attached to the train."

He glanced at the others as he added,

"Of course Francis Knollys will arrange everything as he always does and I am sure you will be able to greet us on Friday evening at about six o'clock."

Robbie went pale but no one noticed.

They were busy planning who they would take with them on the Prince's secret weekend and they all felt that it would certainly be amusing to go to a place none of them had ever visited before.

It was only when he had returned to his lodgings that Robbie wondered what he could do.

For a moment he thought of pretending to be ill or saying the house had burned to the ground or anything else which came into his mind that would prevent the Prince paying him the visit he intended.

Then he told himself he was just being stupid.

After all the house was there, the collection which no one could criticise was in its place, and all he had to do was to make the place habitable for His Royal Highness.

He had gone to bed late and spent most of the dark hours awake until he left London as soon as it was light.

He knew better than anyone else how much there was to do if the Prince was to be entertained as he expected at Creswell Court.

*

But now with his sister staring at him incredulously he found it hard to put into words exactly what he required.

"How can you possibly entertain the Prince here?" Wenda was saying, "unless of course you mean for him just to come for *tea*. I suppose we could clear up the place for tea, if nothing else."

Robbie squared his shoulders.

"The Prince and his friends are coming here for the weekend. I have accepted his hospitality a dozen times already and he even took me with him to Paris."

"Paris!" Wenda cried. "Why did you not tell me?"

"Because I have not been home to do so. I meant to tell you all about it when I came añd now here I am."

"But how can we think about Paris when you have asked the Prince of Wales of all people to be our guest."

"The first thing we have to do," Robbie suggested, "is to supply the house with sufficient servants to make it comfortable."

"And who is going to pay for them?" Wenda asked.

"I will tell you about that later. What we have to do now is to make sure that all the arrangements, which I will tell you about one by one, are carried out. They must all be exactly as the Prince will expect, as I have been received not only in his house but in the houses of his friends."

Wenda made a gesture with her hands and then she sat down on the nearest chair.

"I find it hard to understand what you are saying," she sighed.

At that moment Banks brought in the breakfast and because Robbie was hungry he ate without speaking. He demolished his eggs and bacon and several pieces of toast covered with honey.

Then Wenda queried in a very small voice,

"Are you quite certain we have to do this, Robbie?"

"We have to do it, Wenda, and if we don't, I assure you I will lose the friendship of the Prince of Wales, which I value very highly."

"I understand that, but it's Tuesday morning now and we only have until Friday to get everything done."

It was then that her brother seemed to assume an authority she had never experienced before.

They moved out of the breakfast room and into the study, where they usually sat because it was so small and comfortable.

Robbie went at once to his father's writing desk and sat down, looking in the drawer for some writing paper.

"Now I must make a list," he declared. "It all has to be done of course with whoever is available, but we will be wise to use retired servants like Mrs. Stevenson."

Mrs. Stevenson had been the housekeeper at The Court until she was over seventy and then she had retired to a cottage in the village, but although she was nearing eighty she still walked up to The Court to see Banks.

Wenda knew she was horrified at the way the house had deteriorated since she had left.

"I would suppose Mrs. Stevenson may come back," said Wenda tentatively. "She will only have to supervise and give orders to the maids if we can get them, but I could do that myself."

"I will tell you your position later," Robbie replied and continued,

"I have put down Mrs. Stevenson and we will want at least half-a-dozen maids to clean the rooms and make them as welcome and comfortable as your room."

"And yours," added Wenda. "I have taken a great deal of care to keep the Master bedroom as perfect as it was for Papa."

"That is where His Royal Highness will have to sleep," Robbie stated firmly.

Wenda was about to expostulate then thought better of it – of course if the Prince honoured them by coming to stay at The Court, he should have the best.

Undoubtedly, 'the Master's suite', as it had always been called, was larger and more impressive than any other bedroom in the house.

"How many people are you expecting, Robbie?"

31

She was calculating how many rooms would have to be cleaned out and made habitable.

"There will be twelve including myself. They will be the Duke of Sutherland, Lord Carrington, Lord Charles Beresford and, I expect, the Marquis of Mildenhall. I will find out the names of the ladies and I will tell you which rooms they are all to sleep in."

"They will have to be the rooms we closed up."

"They must all be on the first floor, so that is not difficult."

"Not difficult!" his sister gasped.

"No, we are twelve in all, including me, and as we know there are more rooms than that on the first floor."

"There is my room and I am not giving that up for anyone," Wenda asserted. "I have been in it ever since I came down from the schoolroom when I was fifteen and I refuse to let anyone else spoil it for me."

There was a pause and then Robbie murmured,

"No one will spoil your bedroom, but I am afraid you will have to go away, Wenda!"

"Go away! What on earth do you mean by that?"

"I mean this is a private party ostensibly for men only. As I have not been able to explain to you yet, the Prince and each gentleman brings with him the lady he is currently interested in. And she is *always* a married lady."

Wenda's eyes opened so wide they seemed to fill her whole face.

"I don't understand – "

"I think you do. His Royal Highness wants to be with his special friends and not be bothered by equerries or courtiers."

Wenda was listening wide-eyed and he went on,

"He wishes to relax and enjoy himself and that is what he must be able to do here and what he has found in the homes of his friends where I too have been a visitor."

"Are the ladies they bring with them *really* ladies?" Wenda asked as if she was trying to work it out.

"Of course they are. That is the whole point of the party."

"You said they are all married women. Is that why I am not allowed to be a guest too?"

Her brother nodded.

He was finding it difficult to explain what seemed to him quite a simple equation.

"If I do go away as you want me to do," Wenda added, "you do realise that Mrs. Banks will never be able to manage in the kitchen. Even if the rooms look right, the food will not be good enough without someone to help and instruct her as Mama always did."

"In some houses they employ one of the Prince's favourite chefs. I expect one would be obtainable and I could get in touch with him as soon as I return to London."

Wenda gave a scream of protest.

"Engage a chef! What do you suppose Mrs. Banks would think? It would break her heart. She has looked after us, loved us and cooked for us since you and I were born and managed all the parties Mama and Papa gave."

She drew in her breath before she went on,

"I remember people saying how delicious the food was and how clever of Mama to have such an excellent cook."

There was little point in arguing because Robbie knew this was true.

"Then all I can suggest, Wenda, although you will not like it, is that you stay here in the house and help Mrs. Banks together with any other helpers you may need. But no one must be aware that you are my sister."

To his surprise Wenda smiled at him.

"I am quite prepared to do that rather than being exiled from all the fun, and not even having a glimpse of the Prince or the beautiful women I have read about in the newspapers but thought I would never see."

Her brother stared at her.

"Are you really content to do so?" he asked. "I thought perhaps you would stay with one of our relations."

"If I did, I would not sleep a wink wondering what was happening – if the beds were being made properly and the morning tea brought to the guests in the same way as it was when Mama was alive."

"I think it's very sporting of you, Wenda. Equally I feel it is very mean of me. You know, if it was possible, I would want you to play hostess to the Prince, as Mama would have done."

"I am happy to be in the house and to peep at what is going on and I promise not to interfere. At the same time, Robbie, you know better than I that it is going to be very difficult to get everything ready by Friday."

Robbie looked down at his list.

"I think I had better leave it all to you, Wenda. I thought if you had to go away, I could manage everything. But quite frankly it frightens me as I have no idea how to plan it exactly as His Royal Highness would expect it."

Wenda sat down at the writing table as well and picked up another piece of paper and his pen.

"Now explain to me exactly what you want."

Robbie drew in his breath.

"I have been trying to remember all the details of what is expected and what happened when I stayed with the Devonshires and the Sutherlands."

"I am writing it down, so don't leave anything out."

"First of all His Royal Highness is insistent that we go to great pains to maintain appearances in front of the servants."

Wenda looked up with surprise, but stayed quiet.

"You know as well as I, Wenda, the servants talk and it is very difficult to prevent it."

"Of course it is, but if all those ladies wish to be anonymous here, I don't think they will know very much about them in the village."

"The housemaids will have to dress the ladies, as they don't bring their own maids with them, and serve the meals, make the beds and bring up the bath water.

"It is very important that the bedrooms are all near each other, but that none of the rooms used by the ladies have a connecting door with any adjacent room."

Robbie realised his sister did not really understand why this was necessary, so he went on quickly,

"The names of the ladies must be written on cards and placed in small brass holders on their bedroom doors. A similar card is placed by the bell in the butler's pantry."

"What you mean by small brass holders! There are not any on our doors."

"Well, you could stick the card on the door or fix it with a drawing-pin."

"I suppose it's useful for the servants to know who is in each room," Wenda commented innocently.

Robbie thought it would be a mistake to tell her that it would prevent a man from entering the wrong lady's room by mistake.

He wanted to go over the arrangements with her so that those who wished to be together at night would not have far to walk, but he realised however that she was still not aware of the real reason why each man was bringing a lady with him.

He therefore added rapidly,

"You must make it clear that once dinner has been served and the beds turned down the servants should retire to their own quarters."

"I expect they will anyway, Robbie. Mama never made the servants stay up late. I suppose that the ladies can undo their own dresses when they go to bed."

"I am certain they can manage. Sometimes we are very late and I know Mrs. Stevenson would be too old to stay up."

"Yes, of course she would."

"Oh, and by the way, Wenda, at every house I have stayed at there have been sandwiches and Malvern water by the bed just in case anyone is hungry or thirsty."

"I had forgotten that! But Malvern water is quite expensive."

Robbie knew that they had come back to the main subject which was money.

"I want you to come with me now so that you see what I am going to do and I don't want you to feel later, Wenda, that I have deceived you in any way."

"What are you going to do, Robbie?"

Her brother did not answer.

Instead he now picked up a small case he had been carrying when he left the breakfast room and Wenda then wondered if it contained his night clothes.

Usually when he came home he required nothing and thus did not bother with trunks and everything he left behind in his room was as it had always been and anyway he never stayed long enough to require very much.

Now, carrying the case, he walked through the door of the study and Wenda followed him.

Creswell Court had been rebuilt a hundred years ago and two large wings were added to the main building and in both of these there was a picture gallery.

Even then there were enough pictures to fill the rest of the house and they were certainly very beautiful and very valuable.

Some of them were particularly old, but as Wenda was aware they had been neglected now for far too long for them not to be dusty and the glass over many of them was too dirty to see the picture clearly.

"I suppose you will want these cleaned before the Prince arrives," Wenda asked Robbie as they walked down the corridors.

"I meant to put it on the list, but I think it would be wise for you to have men who are used to pictures rather than those who just bang about and damage them."

"I believe there are some good men in St. Albans who have been used at Hatfield House and Gorhambury, but of course they will be expensive."

Her brother did not answer until he had walked into the West picture gallery and then he asserted,

"Whatever it costs these pictures have to be cleaned and the floor polished."

Wenda had to admit there was a great amount of dust and dirt there now.

"If we have to do this as well as the bedrooms, we will require a dozen or more women from the village."

She was being provocative but he did not respond.

He just walked on until at the end of the gallery he stopped at a picture that Wenda had never really cared for.

It was by Delacroix who had painted it at the very end of the eighteenth century and was entitled '*Still Life with Lobster*' and she had always disliked it – the thought of painting a lobster about to be eaten was unpleasant. But she did appreciate that Delacroix had been a great artist.

To her considerable surprise, having reached '*Still Life with Lobster*' Robbie was lifting it down.

"What are you going to do with it?" she asked him.

"I can tell you exactly what I am going to do with it and with another picture I am taking away with me. I am going to have it copied."

"*Copied*! But you can't do that?"

"Of course I can, Wenda, and it will be so skilfully done that the Trustees even if they look at it at all carefully, which I rather doubt, will have not the slightest idea it is not the original."

Wenda looked at him in horror.

"And what are you doing with the original?" she quizzed in little more than a whisper.

"I am selling it. I am fed up to the teeth of living in this appalling hole-in-the-corner way, having to consider every penny we spend while there are thousands of pounds hanging on our walls and we are too poor even to invite people to admire them!"

"But they are entailed," Wenda cried out. "All the pictures are entailed to your son when you have one."

"I am as likely to be able to afford to have a son as to fly over the moon. I have not lived recently with all these rich people without realising how expensive life is if you want any comforts and enjoyments. I am in debt, the house is in debt and so is the estate."

38

He paused dramatically before he added,

"Well, I am going to pay that off and if my son, if I ever have one, finds out he has been looking at a copy of the original, then I can only say he will understand I could not carry on any longer defrauding the bank and everyone else simply because I had no money."

Robbie spoke forcefully and she realised because she knew him so well that it was an issue that rankled him so much and he could bear it no longer.

"Suppose the Trustees should find out, Robbie," she whispered.

"Unless I am more stupid than I appear, I have no intention of being taken to task over my own pictures. No one will know what has happened except you and before the copy returns it is impossible that anyone who visits this gallery or the other will realise each is one picture short."

There was nothing Wenda could say.

Carrying the picture she then followed her brother without speaking to the East gallery added by their great-grandfather to give him room for ever more art.

Here were many pictures that Wenda particularly loved, including Rubens '*Joy of the Regent*' and she had adored the small naked children running about ever since she was old enough to look at them.

She breathed a sigh of relief that her brother passed this one as well as the lovely '*Diana the Huntress*' which she had often thought of when she herself was out shooting with her father.

He stopped at Baugin's '*Le Dessert Gaufrettes*'. The artist had been born in 1630 and it was a picture of a glass of wine and a plate of wafers which she had always considered rather dull.

Wenda had preferred the work of the older Masters such as Boucher's '*Diana Resting after her Bath*' and she thought if Robbie was going to take away that particular Boucher she would have cried.

As it was she was terrified he would be caught.

There would be a hideous row with the Trustees if they discovered that he had broken the entail.

"Are you certain," she asked him, "that no one will know you have taken these?"

"The only person who will know, as far as I am concerned, is the artist I met in Paris who is a genius at copying old Masters. He took me and His Royal Highness up to his studio where there were a number of copies of paintings in the Louvre. It was impossible for a non-expert to realise they had not been painted two centuries earlier.

"As his Royal Highness pointed out to me, it was extremely clever of him to obtain canvases of the right age for the works he had copied."

"And you can trust him, Robbie?"

"He trusted *me*. In fact because I was with the Prince he has already advanced me five hundred pounds on the pictures I promised him, and he hopes to give me one thousand more when he sells them to collectors who keep secret where they have bought their latest pieces."

There was a faint twist to his lips as he added,

"And he makes a fortune this way, I assure you."

"Five hundred pounds would certainly pay for the weekend, and please can I pay Donson's wages out of it until you have time to sell my brooch?"

"We are not selling your brooch until we absolutely have to. I will give you most of the money now so that you can pay those we employ for the Royal visit."

"I will not only have to pay them but I will require money for food."

"I know that, Wenda, and I will have to bring some fine wine down from London."

By this time they had reached the hall and Robbie put the pictures down before he felt in his pocket.

He drew out three hundred pounds and counted it slowly into Wenda's hand.

"That should be enough," he said. "I need the rest to pay a debt I dare not leave any longer and for the wine."

"You are leaving now, Robbie?"

"I am afraid so. As a matter of fact I have someone to meet who is taking the two pictures to Paris for me and I have promised to go racing with His Royal Highness."

He gave a deep sigh before he added,

"I am only so grateful that I can leave everything in your capable hands, my dearest sister, when I was afraid I would have to stay myself and oversee it all."

"I will do my very best, but you do realise, Robbie, it is not going to be easy to get everything done in time."

"However difficult it is, it has to be done," he said firmly.

Wenda glanced at the grandfather clock which was standing inside the front door.

"It is almost luncheon time and Mrs. Banks will, I know, have been cooking you a meal. After all the horses must have a rest and I suggest that the groom who came with you will be hungry too."

Robbie laughed.

"You are right, Wenda, I am over-anxious and of course feeling nervous. So much depends on this party that naturally I am afraid things may go wrong."

"That is not the way to look at it, remember Mama always said, 'believe things will be right and they come right'."

"They are already coming right because it is you who is helping me, Wenda."

She was so touched at his reply that she felt tears coming into her eyes.

"I love you, Robbie," she sighed, "and I have been very lonely while you were away for so long."

"I feel ashamed of myself, but I have been growing up and finding the world a very different place from what I expected."

He looked down at the two pictures.

"I would not have dared a year ago to do what I am doing now. But I suppose being with the Prince has made me give myself airs!"

"I think they are very becoming, but don't let them blow away in a hostile wind!"

Her brother kissed her cheek.

"You are a brick, Wenda, now run and fetch me something to pack these pictures in so that no one can see them and by tomorrow morning they will be in France."

"I think you have changed, Robbie. You are far more of a man than when you left home. In fact I can quite understand why you are such a success in London and you must find us very dull here at The Court."

"I admit that I have neglected you disgracefully, but it will not happen again. I will somehow make enough money, however crooked it may be, to give you what you are entitled to – a Season in London. And I will expect you to marry, if not the Prince of Wales, as he is already married, then someone equally important!"

Wenda laughed.

"'*If wishes were horses, beggars might ride*'," she quoted, "and that is something we all have to remember."

"If I have anything to do with it, I have no intention of being a beggar any longer. It gives one an inferiority complex and that I have vowed to myself never to have again."

"I will find you a cover for the pictures and I will pray that they arrive safely in Paris and no one notices the two gaps on the walls in the galleries."

"The only people likely to notice it are the ghosts of our ancestors and if they are angry with us, then I will just have to placate them by starting a new collection of my own. Who knows, I may uncover something the Creswells have not discovered before?"

By the time he had finished speaking Wenda had run up the stairs and in the linen cupboard she found some dark silk bedspreads. She realised that if the pictures were wrapped in them, the package would not arouse suspicion as to what it might contain.

Only as she carried them down to her brother did she realise what a task he had set her and she wondered if she would be able to carry it through.

Then she told herself if their ancestors had played brave parts in a thousand different ways in the history of England, she and Robbie must be brave too – even though at the moment it was not all plain sailing.

'But we have the Prince of Wales coming to stay,' she told herself, 'and who can ask more of fate than that?'

CHAPTER THREE

Once luncheon was finished Robbie drove quickly back to London.

The horses were rather tired and he did not make such good time as on the outward journey. He had hired the hackney carriage, but as the coachman knew he was a good driver, he was allowed to take the reins himself.

He could not help thinking as he drove that as soon as he could afford it he would buy some decent horses and a new carriage.

When Robbie arrived in London he went straight to the house of his friend, Mr. Hudson.

And it was he who had given him the name of the painter in Paris whose studio he had visited with His Royal Highness and Robbie had met him at Marlborough House.

When he realised that Robbie had one of the finest collections in England, he had become very friendly and asked him to dinner.

His house was exactly what Robbie expected and it was filled with pictures like his own.

As they became friends, it was impossible for Mr. Hudson not to learn how hard-up Robbie was and just how difficult it was for him to keep the house and the estate going with practically no income.

It was then that Mr. Hudson had told him about the artist in Paris.

He had not actually advised Robbie to use him – he just hinted that if things were desperate Robbie could have one or two of his pictures copied and done so well that the Trustees would have no idea they were not the originals.

It was therefore to Mr. Hudson that he had turned and confided in him that his affairs were indeed desperate and he would be in terrible trouble if he could not afford to pay his debts.

And what was more he would lose his friendship with the Prince of Wales.

Mr. Hudson had perused with him the catalogue of the pictures at Creswell Court and chosen two pictures.

As a first attempt it would be wise to choose those pictures that were not so outstanding and did not instantly catch the eye of anyone entering the picture galleries.

When Robbie drew up at his house, Mr. Hudson himself came out and helped him carry in the two precious pictures and they put them down in the sitting room.

Mr. Hudson then carefully started to remove the silk bedspread covering the pictures.

"So you have done it, my boy!" he said to Robbie, "and I hope that no one at your house will talk."

"The only person who has the slightest idea of what we are doing is my sister, Wenda, and I would trust her with my life."

"Of course you can," Mr. Hudson said reassuringly, "and you can be quite certain that these pictures will make you a lot of money."

He was standing beside Delacroix's *Still Life with Lobster* and went on,

"Just look at this! Have you ever seen such superb painting?"

Robbie did not speak, but started to undo the other picture and he had been rather surprised that Mr. Hudson had asked him to bring '*Le Dessert Gaufrettes*' when he had seen it in the catalogue. He agreed with Wenda that it was a rather dull picture.

As if he had spoken aloud Mr. Hudson told him,

"In the last Exhibition of Baugin's pictures in Paris, the prices soared up to the sky. I will be very surprised if this does not fetch more than your Delacroix."

"I am only too willing to believe you – "

Mr. Hudson looked at the time.

"I am expecting a yacht to arrive from France at about six o'clock. I suggest you and I have a drink, then we will take these pictures to the river and speed them on their way as soon as possible."

Robbie agreed happily and they drank champagne before Mr. Hudson's carriage appeared. It was closed and the two pictures were quickly carried in and put on the seat opposite where they would sit.

And then they set off and Robbie thought excitedly that, as he had told Wenda, the pictures would be in France by the morning.

They drove some way along the Embankment until they were almost at the Tower of London and then the carriage came to a standstill at a deserted spot.

Mr. Hudson climbed out and stood looking up and down the Thames and then called over to Robbie,

"We are early and of course the crossing may have been rough, which always delays even the most expensive yacht."

As he finished speaking, Mr. Hudson gave a cry,

"Here he comes! I can see the yacht rounding the far bend of the river. You will have to admit it's a smart little number."

Robbie climbed out of the carriage and they both walked to the edge of the river.

Now Robbie saw that coming towards them was a small but well-proportioned yacht that he would love to own himself.

He had accompanied the Prince of Wales when he had visited Cowes last year and had been entranced by the fine yachts assembled there and because he was with His Royal Highness he was able to go aboard most of them.

This was another toy he longed to be rich enough to possess.

It took a little time for the French yacht to reach them on the river's edge and as soon as the gangway was slid down, Mr. Hudson and Robbie went aboard.

A short middle-aged Frenchman was there waiting to meet them and Mr. Hudson introduced him as the Comte de Laufé, who piped up at once,

"We have had an excellent crossing. In fact I think I have broken my own record by about twenty minutes!"

Mr. Hudson laughed.

"You will surely infuriate the owners of the English yachts which I can assure you take longer than yours! I am delighted to see you again, Jacques."

"As I am delighted to see you," the Comte replied. "I suppose as usual you expect me to do some of your dirty work for you. I told Sula before we left I was bringing him something to warm his heart."

"That is true enough, Jacques."

As they were talking the Comte was leading them into the Saloon, where there was a bottle of champagne already opened and a plate of pâté sandwiches.

"Sit down and make yourselves comfortable," the Comte ordered, "while my men bring your pictures aboard and stow them safely."

Mr. Hudson and Robbie obeyed him with alacrity.

"If they are as good as you usually give me," the Comte continued, "they will have a cabin to themselves and every attention until they are in Sula's hands."

"You know how grateful I am to you for all you have done for me," said Mr. Hudson, "and Lord Creswell will, I know, be more delighted than he can express once Sula has finished his work in his usual exquisite fashion."

"You can be quite sure of that," the Comte agreed. "But now I have done something for you, I want you to do something for me."

Mr. Hudson spread out his hands.

"All I have is yours," he said mimicking the Arabs.

"I was just about to leave Ostend when a charming married lady begged my help. She was in a hurry to reach London and the very least I could do in the circumstances was to offer to bring her here in my yacht."

Mr. Hudson raised his eyebrows.

"I thought you disliked passengers, Jacques."

"It's true but I could not be unkind to this particular lady and I feel, having done my best to help her, I can now leave her in your hands."

"Of course, I will take her wherever she wishes to go," Mr. Hudson agreed.

As he spoke a Steward entered to fill their glasses and the Comte said to him in French,

"Ask Madame Frazer to join us."

The Steward nodded and they heard him go below.

"Have you any idea who this lady is?" Mr. Hudson enquired.

"She is not at all talkative and I never press people to confide in me. I invariably find it is either an expensive action or a tiresome one!"

They laughed at his remark and then the Steward opened the door of the Saloon and a woman entered.

From the way the Comte had spoken, Robbie was expecting to see someone getting on towards middle age, yet doubtless smart and voluble as all Frenchwomen were.

At the first glance the woman coming somewhat shyly in to join them seemed to be little more than a girl.

She was absolutely one of the prettiest girls Robbie had ever seen.

She had dark hair and large surprisingly blue eyes and instead of the darker hue of most Frenchwomen, a pale pink and white skin.

As she came into the Saloon there was a moment's pause before the three gentlemen rose to their feet.

"Now, Madame Frazer," the Comte began, "I am anxious for you to meet Mr. Hudson and Lord Creswell."

The two of them shook hands with Madame Frazer who gave them each a small nervous smile.

Robbie felt that she was either extremely shy or, for some reason he could not ascertain, frightened.

"Now that I have brought you here safely," the Comte was saying, "you only have to tell Mr. Hudson where you would like to go and his carriage is waiting to take you there."

It was quite obvious the Comte did not wish them to stay any longer so Mr. Hudson held out his hand.

"Thank you, Jacques, for being so helpful as you always are. I am very grateful and I know my friend Lord Creswell feels the same."

"I do indeed," agreed Robbie. "And I know what has been brought aboard will be safe with you."

"You can be sure of that," came in the Comte, "and I am returning immediately. In fact I have an appointment tomorrow evening in Paris that I have no wish to miss."

49

"Then we must not keep you," Mr. Hudson added, "and thank you again a thousand times."

He walked out of the Saloon with the Comte as he was speaking and Robbie turned to Madame Frazer.

"Where would you like to go?" he asked her.

"I don't – know," she replied in a small voice.

It was the first time she had spoken.

Robbie looked at her with surprise.

"You mean you are not staying with friends?"

"I have never been to London before, but perhaps you can find me a nice quiet hotel."

Robbie was astonished. Looking at Madame Frazer she appeared to be very young and certainly not at all sure of herself and he did notice a gold wedding ring on her left hand. It seemed extraordinary she should arrive in London without knowing where she was to stay or having friends to meet her.

Of course there were a number of hotels to which he could take her, but she was entirely alone and the very best hotels did not encourage single ladies, especially when they were young and attractive.

There were many other hotels of which Robbie had very little knowledge, but she might find the other visitors there unpleasant or seeing how she looked, too familiar.

By this time they had reached the carriage and Mr. Hudson was once again thanking the Comte for his help.

They climbed in and as the carriage moved off and they waved goodbye to the Comte, Mr. Hudson declared,

"I have told my coachman to drop me at my Club. Then, Robbie, I would suggest you take Madame Frazer to wherever she wishes to go and then the carriage is yours."

"That is very kind of you."

Robbie guessed that Mr. Hudson thought he would be going to a smart party, as he usually did, perhaps one at Marlborough House.

There was in fact seldom an evening when Robbie did not have an invitation to a dinner party or a ball.

As it happened, before he left London, because he was in such a hurry to reach The Court, he had made no arrangements and he was not even sure without returning to his lodging if he had an invitation for tonight.

When they drove off he turned to Madame Frazer,

"Now we have to tell the driver where to go and I am rather worried as to where I can advise you to stay."

"Please will you find me – somewhere quiet – and respectable," replied Madame Frazer.

Robbie smiled at her.

"Strangely enough that is a difficult problem."

"There must be – somewhere."

She was now looking distinctly worried and Robbie thought it would only make matters worse if he explained to her she looked too young and too pretty to stay alone in most London hotels.

She might easily get into trouble if the hotel catered for a certain type of man such as commercial travellers or ne'er-do-wells who would look on a pretty woman alone as 'fair game'.

"Is this really the first time you have ever been to London?" Robbie asked her tentatively.

"I have been living in France – and I have therefore never had the opportunity before."

"And your husband is not travelling with you?"

There was a moment's pause as she looked away from him and then she said,

"My h-husband is – dead."

"I am so sorry."

He realised as she spoke that she had stumbled over the word 'husband' and it suddenly occurred to him that she did not look in the least like a married woman – nor in fact did she seem old enough to be one.

The carriage was moving on and Robbie knew that soon they would be nearing Mayfair, so he suggested,

"It will be very difficult at this time of night to find you somewhere where you will be both comfortable and safe. As it happens, in the house where I lodge a friend of mine has left today for the country. I suggest that you stay for tonight in my flat, where you will be quite comfortable, while I can use my friend's without any problems."

Madame Frazer's eyes lit up.

"Do you really mean it?" she asked. "You are very kind – I came to London in a great hurry and did not make any plans – but it seems so much bigger than I expected."

Robbie laughed.

"I can understand you feeling like that, especially at this time of the evening. Tomorrow you may find you have friends you forgot about and who you can stay with."

She replied to him in her soft voice,

"I would be very grateful – to stay somewhere near you tonight."

Robbie thought it was a strange thing to say, but did not comment on it. He knocked on the little glass door so that he could speak to the coachman.

"Take me to number 10 Mount Street," he ordered.

The coachman touched his hat.

"Very good, my Lord."

It did not take long and Madame Frazer listened attentively as Robbie pointed out the sights of London.

They drew up outside No. 10 and the footman on the box opened the carriage door and took a small case from the back of the carriage.

Robbie realised that it was Madame's luggage.

"Is this all you have?" he asked her.

Most women travelled with an enormous amount of trunks and hatboxes.

"I came away – in a hurry," she answered simply.

The footman set down her case as the front door was opened by a porter.

"Evenin', my Lord," he addressed Robbie.

"This lady will be staying in my flat this evening, Jenkins, and I will be using Mr. Armstrong's."

"Very good, my Lord. Shall I take this case up to your flat?"

"Yes, it is Madame's."

The porter went on ahead of them up the stairs and reached the second floor where Robbie's flat was situated.

It consisted of two small rooms and a bathroom and he had found it quite comfortable and cheap compared with other places he certainly could not afford.

What was important was to be in Mayfair and to be in the centre of Society as he could usually walk to dinner parties and balls and this saved him money.

Madame Frazer now looked round the sitting room which was decorated mostly with Robbie's books. There was a writing desk and a table, both of Regency design, that had come from Creswell Court.

"This is very pretty," she murmured.

"It is not very large, but it is my home in London."

Robbie looked at the grandfather clock as he said,

"They do not provide food here with the exception of breakfast. I hope when you have had a little rest you will allow me to take you out to dinner."

Madame Frazer's eyes lit up.

"Are you sure you don't have a prior engagement?"

"I should be delighted if you would dine with me," Robbie insisted.

"That will be so lovely for me. It would be rather sad to spend my first night in London alone and unable to have anything to eat."

Robbie laughed.

"I will take you out for dinner and we will have a nice simple meal in nearby Shepherd's Market."

"That will be wonderful," she sighed. "Thank you – very very much."

He then showed her the bedroom and the bathroom which was small but at least convenient.

"I will come back for you at half-past eight. I am sure after crossing the Channel you should lie down for at least an hour."

"As you have been so kind I will be too excited to go to sleep and I would hate – to keep you waiting."

"If you need anything," Robbie told her, "you can ask the porter or else knock on the door along the corridor which is where I will be sleeping in my friend's flat."

"You are so kind I don't know how to thank you."

He took his evening clothes and then left her alone. He went into his friend's flat which was almost identical to his, except that it was not so well furnished.

He felt that there was some mystery about Madame Frazer which was intriguing. It seemed extraordinary that someone who was obviously a lady and well-bred should, even if she was indeed a widow, be allowed to travel alone – without a courier, without a lady's-maid and apparently without a friend.

'There is certainly something odd about her,' he said to himself, 'and it will interest me to find out the truth and what is behind Madame's hurried trip to London.'

As he had his bath and changed, he thought it was the sort of story the Prince of Wales would enjoy and he would also be only too eager to meet someone so beautiful and apparently friendless.

It passed through Robbie's mind that, if His Royal Highness had been in his position, he would not have left his own flat for that of his friend.

Then Robbie told himself that Madame Frazer was too young to understand the risk she was taking in going alone to a country she had never visited before – or else she was an adventuress who expected to be involved in a dream of some sort.

Judging by her looks she would not be very long in finding it.

There was a place in Shepherd's Market where the food was good and single gentlemen, like Robbie, ate there if they did not go to their Club.

When Robbie knocked on the door of his sitting room, Madame Frazer's soft voice answered him.

He opened the door and saw that she was wearing a very pretty and fashionable gown and he knew at a glance it must have come from Paris and was very expensive.

She looked even lovelier than when he had first seen her.

Her dark hair was most elegantly arranged and he thought that with her strange piercing blue eyes she was so exceptionally beautiful that it would have been dangerous for her to dine alone – even in a respectable hotel.

Robbie looked his best in his evening clothes and she looked at him appreciatively.

For a moment they just gazed at each other instead of speaking and then she said in the soft frightened voice she had used before,

"It is very kind of you to take me out to dinner. I don't want to be an encumbrance, but if I was alone I would have no idea where to go."

"Of course not and in case no one has told you, you should never walk about alone in London, especially in the evening."

She did not answer and so he added,

"You know that is true in Paris and in every large City. So you must take great care of yourself."

She smiled at him.

"It is so thrilling for me to be in London. I have always wanted to come here."

"I only hope you are not disappointed. As we are going to walk to the restaurant, you will need a wrap."

"I packed so quickly," she said almost as if he had asked the question, "that I forgot I would want a cape in the evening. Just in case you are kind enough to ask me out to dinner again, I had better buy one tomorrow."

It passed through his mind that she was obviously not short of money, although when he was dressing, it had occurred to him that if he had taken her to a hotel, she might have wanted him to pay the bill.

Now he saw that she was wearing a string of pearls round her neck that were obviously valuable. And there was a bracelet on her wrist – if the stones were real, which he felt sure they were, it was a costly piece of jewellery – in which case surely she must have friends who would invite her to stay with them.

As she was English, why not English relations?

There was however, he thought, just a faint accent in the way she pronounced some words.

It was not entirely the usual way an English lady of Society would have spoken, but, as she had lived abroad, she might have had to speak French all the time.

Then she could have acquired a faint French accent which would alter some words – it was all a riddle which he was determined to solve.

They set off down Mount Street into Curzon Street and within a few minutes they were in Shepherd's Market.

Opening out of Curzon Street it was a picturesque part of London, reminiscent of Montmartre, with its open-air flower market, tall red chimneys and red-tiled roofs.

The head-waiter welcomed Robbie with obvious delight,

"You've been neglecting us, my Lord," he began. "But I expect it's because there're so many parties you never have time to enjoy a quiet dinner here with us."

"I am with you now," Robbie replied, "and I have brought a very lovely lady who is as hungry as I am. So tell us what you have on the menu for tonight."

He showed them to a comfortable corner.

The restaurant was by no means smart, but Robbie had enjoyed a great number of meals there either alone or with a friend.

Yet never, he reflected, had he been with anyone quite so attractive as his companion tonight.

After he had ordered from the menu, he began,

"Now do tell me about yourself, Madame Frazer. You can imagine how curious I am, as I had no idea, nor had Mr. Hudson, that the Comte would be bringing anyone with him from France."

"It was very kind of him to let me travel with him, and I was surprised how quickly his yacht could move. Far quicker than – ours."

As she spoke the last words she seemed to realise she had made a mistake and added quickly,

"I mean – my h-husband's."

She stammered again over the word 'husband' and Robbie remarked,

"Your relations in France must be aware, as I am, that you are far too beautiful, and in fact far too young, to move about the world unchaperoned and unprotected."

Because he had paid her a compliment Madame Frazer blushed and she looked even more irresistible than before and Robbie was even more convinced that she was indeed very young.

He bent forward.

"If we are to be friends and quite frankly you need a friend, then we must be honest with each other."

There was silence and then Madame Frazer said,

"Please, I don't want – to tell anyone who I am – or why I am here."

The very idea seemed to make her tremble.

"But you cannot fight the world alone. If you have committed a murder or some other crime, I will help and protect you, I promise."

"You are so kind. I did not believe there was so much kindness in the world especially from people one has never met before."

"Are you telling me you do not know the Comte?"

"I know him only by name and when he agreed to take me to London, he did not insist on my explaining why I was going there or who I am."

Robbie smiled.

"So you told him you are Madame Frazer. I know you said your husband is dead, but I doubt if there was ever a Monsieur Frazer to call himself your husband!"

Her eyes flickered and she looked away from him.

"Why – did you say – that?" she asked in a voice that shook.

"Because you look too young to be married and so beautiful that no man, unless he was blind, deaf and dumb, would allow you to run away alone."

"Do you think – I look as if I am running away?"

"But of course I do. If you had a real husband and I don't believe he ever existed, he would not only never let you leave him but he would certainly be on the next ship crossing the Channel to find you!"

There was silence.

He thought with her head turned away from him that she was as lovely as any Greek Goddess and it would be impossible for a man who once possessed her to ever let her go.

As softly as she had spoken, he asked her again,

"Do tell me the truth. Tell me about yourself and I promise to help you in any way I can and of course protect you. To be frank, you will need it."

Again there was a long silence until she whispered in a voice he could hardly hear,

"I want to trust you – but if I do – I am afraid that you will insist on my going back to France."

"I would have no authority to give you any orders," replied Robbie. "I am only asking you to trust me so that I can try to help you and protect you from getting into more trouble than you are in already."

She drew in her breath and still did not speak and after a moment Robbie persisted,

"Tell me please, what is your real name. I cannot go on calling you 'Madame Frazer' which I am sure you are not entitled to."

She gave a little laugh before she answered,

"I was christened Josofine – "

"Very well, Josofine, and the name does suit you. My name is Robbie. So tell me why you have run away."

"You are quite sure – I have?"

"Quite sure. You could not look as you do, dress as you do and act as you do unless you had someone to run away from."

She laughed and it was a very pretty sound.

"You make it sound so funny. Yes, I had to run away otherwise I would have been forced to marry a man I thought was really horrible."

Robbie felt suddenly relieved.

Although he would not admit it even to himself, he had been afraid there really was a Monsieur Frazer on the warpath.

"So you ran away from Paris, Josofine?"

She nodded.

"It was the only thing I could do. My parents were determined I should marry that man. And as you know, marriages in France are arranged."

Robbie thought that this only happened amongst the aristocracy.

"If the man your parents wanted you to marry really disgusted you, then you did the only thing you could do."

Josofine gave a little cry.

"Oh, that is wonderful, you *do* understand! If I had stayed I would have found myself walking up the aisle however much I protested against it."

She gave a deep sigh.

"I heard that the Comte was leaving for England – they were talking about it last night at dinner. So I just packed what I needed in a light case I could carry myself and set out for Ostend while it was still dark."

"How did you do that?"

"I walked to a Posting inn which is not far from my home. I reached Ostend just in time to find the Comte and beg him to take me aboard before he left for England."

She gave a little laugh.

"Actually he was still asleep when I arrived there – so I waited in the Saloon until he came up for breakfast."

"It must have given him a great shock to find you looking so glorious and demanding a passage when he least expected it."

Josofine laughed again.

"I had heard he did not like having passengers with him and preferred being entirely alone except for the crew on his yacht. Yet when I pleaded with him, he gave in."

Robbie mused, seeing how lovely she was, it would be difficult for any man to refuse her anything she asked.

"Now you have arrived in England, Josofine, and you are apparently friendless, what do you intend to do?"

Josofine gave what was undoubtedly a very French shrug of her shoulders.

"I expect," she said, "eventually I will have to go home. But by that time the horrible man they want me to marry will have gone away and I hope they will realise once and for all I will *not* marry anyone I do not love."

"That is going to be somewhat difficult for you living in France," suggested Robbie.

"I know," Josofine replied. "In which case I will just have to stay with you, whether you want me or not!"

Naturally she was joking.

But it suddenly struck Robbie that it would be an unexpected and very welcome gift from the Gods.

"One thing we must do," he said aloud, "is to make plans. As I would want you to enjoy yourself on this mad escapade, I will show you London, so that when you go home it will be something for you to remember."

Josofine gave a cry of delight.

"Oh, that is what I want. I want to go to the Zoo. I want to see the British Museum, the Tower of London and of course Buckingham Palace."

"That is quite enough," countered Robbie, "to keep us busy for a week at least."

With a jerk Robbie suddenly remembered that on Friday afternoon the Prince of Wales and his friends were all arriving at Creswell Court.

And then he was also aware that he had not yet told Francis Knollys who he would be bringing with him to the secret party that was to take place at his home.

He had been overcome with horror at what needed to be done before the party arrived, and had therefore not given a thought to the fact that he would have to produce a partner – just as all the other gentlemen in the party would be providing their own special and secretive ladies.

Looking at Josofine he thought how interesting it would be to show her his own home and his pictures and if Wenda had done her job well they would be worth seeing.

'We will talk about that later,' he mused.

At the same time the thought persisted in his mind all through dinner.

They talked of where they would go tomorrow and decided to visit first the Zoo and the Tower of London.

"I want to see everything, but everything," Josofine was saying in a rapt voice as dinner ended, "but please I don't want to be a bore so that you feel obliged to look after me when you have a thousand other things to do."

"I cannot think of anything more important at the moment than looking after you. It is all such an exciting adventure and just so unexpected that I am half afraid that when I wake up tomorrow morning, I will find I have been dreaming and you have disappeared into thin air or gone back to France!"

"I am certainly not going to do that, Robbie. The most wonderful thing that could possibly happen is that I have found you and you should be so kind to me."

"I think you would find quite a few men prepared to do so," Robbie added cynically.

"If they were French, they would have frightened me, but because you are English and you understand, *you* are different from anyone else."

Robbie smiled at her, but he could not understand how she was working that out in her mind, although at the same time he hoped he would always be able to live up to her expectations and not scare her.

She slipped her arm into his as they walked back to Mount Street later in the evening.

It was only a short distance, but there were men standing about at the street corners who looked somehow sinister.

As they passed them, Robbie felt Josofine move a little nearer to him and he knew she was thinking that if she had been alone she would have been intimidated.

'She is little more than a child,' he told himself, 'and I must be very careful not to make her nervous of me as she is of other men.'

He had deliberately not questioned her any further about her parents and the man she was running away from. He felt certain that sooner or later she would tell him of her own free will.

Equally he could not help still feeling curious.

She was so lovely and he was experienced enough to know that her clothes were very expensive. They could only have been made by a Parisian couturier of the highest grade.

Her jewellery was real and she was certainly not suffering from poverty.

He could not understand why she was being forced to marry a man the thought of whom made her tremble.

The reason must have been that he was rich enough to make the arranged marriage particularly acceptable to her parents.

They arrived at his flat and then as a sleepy porter let them in, they walked upstairs.

"It has been a delightful evening," sighed Josofine, "and thank you for being so kind to me, Robbie."

She looked up at him.

And he wanted as he had never wanted anything in his life before to kiss her.

Then he recognised that it was far too soon.

It might be something he would be able to do later without frightening her.

So instead he picked up her hand and bent over it in the French fashion.

"Goodnight, Josofine. Sleep well and tomorrow we will start our sightseeing tour which I hope you will find fascinating."

"Please can we breakfast together?" she asked him.

"Yes, of course. I will tell the porter and I think we should make it nine o'clock so that you will have plenty of time for your beauty sleep."

Josofine gave a little laugh.

"As I don't want you to be ashamed of me, I will certainly sleep until half-past eight."

Robbie turned towards the door.

"Goodnight," he said again, "and promise me you will not fly away in the middle of the night, so that in the morning I will find it has all been a dream."

"I promise you I will be here, but I shall be afraid, if you are not here at nine o'clock, that you have changed your mind."

"I will not do that," Robbie promised her.

He closed the door and heard her very sensibly turn the key in the lock.

As he walked to his friend's flat, Robbie thought that never in his life had he met anyone so intriguing or so enthralling as Josofine.

CHAPTER FOUR

At Creswell Court Wenda was astonished at how quickly events were moving.

By Wednesday the whole house was beginning to look quite different.

It was mainly due to Banks and Mrs. Stevenson and they were thrilled at the whole idea of his Lordship holding a house party.

Wenda was careful not to say who was coming.

She knew however that the news of a party, which had not taken place at The Court for so long, delighted the village.

In fact Banks could have had a dozen more footmen than he required, but he was wise enough to choose young men who were better educated and therefore likely to be more efficient than the ordinary villager.

Mrs. Stevenson in the meantime engaged women she knew personally and they were very pleased at having the opportunity for work if only for a short while.

It seemed to Wenda after months of being alone with only the Bankses to look after her and the house, that she was now living in a new world.

It was actually organised turmoil.

When she came down the stairs in the morning, the maids were already hard at it washing the floors, scrubbing the mantelpieces and shaking the carpets.

In every room she looked in there seemed to be half a dozen women doing something and she could only hope the money Robbie had given her would be enough to pay everyone as they certainly earned every penny and a great deal more.

They enjoyed the excitement of being at The Court and many of them had never been inside the house before and they competed with each other to get the work done.

Wenda concentrated on the pictures, but she soon found there were too many for her, so she therefore had to ask the experts from St. Albans for help.

In three days she found it hard to recognise her own home. Everything in the house was shining brightly and everything looked somehow different.

Wenda was determined for Robbie's sake that his smart friends would not sneer at what they saw – or to have any grounds to be able to find fault and claim that they were uncomfortable.

The special rooms she chose for the guests were all State bedrooms and they were all on the same floor as her brother had insisted.

She did not question why they should want to be all together – she merely took it for granted.

Only sometimes when she was lying in bed did she shiver at the thought that the Prince of Wales was coming. He might find it very different here from the other grand houses he normally stayed in.

Now that Robbie had explained to her how often he was with His Royal Highness she could understand.

Of course he wanted to make his home as good as, if not better, than others he had been invited to with the Prince.

She did not quite understand about the ladies.

Why did they want to have their names emblazoned on their doors?

Then she thought it must be a new custom she had not heard of before.

There was no word from Robbie as to what names she was to write on the cards and she thought it would be tiresome of him if he brought the list with him when he arrived – it would mean she had to do everything in a hurry at the last moment.

She was therefore delighted to receive a letter from Robbie on Thursday morning.

He gave her a list of the guests, without of course writing in the name of His Royal Highness.

*

Robbie had spent the first two days sightseeing with Josofine, which he had not done since he was small.

They had gone first to the Zoo and then on to the Tower of London and finally to Madame Tussaud's and they had been surprised to find that the day was practically over and there was no time to do anymore.

"It has been wonderful, wonderful!" Josofine cried, clasping her hands together. "I have enjoyed it so much!"

She paused to look at him questioningly before she asked,

"I hope it has not bored you, Robbie?"

"How can I be bored when I am with you – ?"

Robbie loved the faint colour that then came into her cheeks and the way her eyes looked shyly away.

He knew that every moment he was becoming more attached to her and he now found her even more alluring than he had at first and he could not explain to himself why she was so different.

Except that she was certainly more beautiful than any woman he had ever met before.

She behaved in a very different way from anyone else and primarily it was because she made no effort to flirt with him as the elite of Mayfair had done ever since he arrived in London.

He was used to the invitation in their eyes and on their lips and the way their hands would touch his as if accidentally – and there was nothing accidental about it.

He enjoyed himself in the same way as the Prince of Wales always did. He made love to the women whose husbands were away shooting, fishing or racing.

He was not interested in the *debutantes* and young girls, who were only concerned with getting married and although he could not afford a wife, he had a title and there were always ambitious Mamas who wanted their daughter called 'my Lady' after she had walked down the aisle on her husband's arm.

Because Josofine was so unlike the other women he had known, Robbie too behaved in a different way towards her and not as he would have behaved with a married woman aware of every twist and turn of the game.

Josofine was like a child.

She was thrilled with the Zoo, and when the tigers roared at her she slipped her hand into his – not because she was being flirtatious, but because she felt she needed his protection.

His fingers closed over hers and yet he sensed that she was more fascinated by the tigers and she was not thinking of him in any way except that he was there to take care of her.

Josofine was now busy making a list of the places she wanted to visit the following day.

While she did so, he wrote to the hostesses whose invitations he had accepted that week and asked them to forgive him for not being able to be their guest as he had promised at a dinner or a ball – unfortunately he had to go to the country and it was an explanation they would accept.

So it was essential at this stage that he should not be seen in London by them or one of their friends.

Fortunately, as Josofine was so keen on sightseeing, the members of the *Beau Monde* were not likely to be visiting the Tower of London which had so delighted her nor indeed spending hours in the National Portrait Gallery examining with delight its endless pictures.

It was on Wednesday that he remembered he had not called at Marlborough House to be given the names of those who had been invited to His Royal Highness's secret weekend at Creswell Court.

Robbie thought it wise if he went there at luncheon time, when he was almost sure His Royal Highness would be out either with a lady he was particularly attracted to or attending some large luncheon given in his honour.

Robbie had no wish to meet the Prince at present in case he questioned him as to who he was bringing to his own party.

Francis Knollys was in his usual office and looked up smiling when he appeared.

"I wondered what had happened to you, my Lord," he said. "In fact last night His Royal Highness was asking me if I had seen you. He was disappointed you were not at the party he had just attended."

"You must tell His Royal Highness that I was in the country getting my house shipshape for his visit!"

"I felt that was the reason. Of course His Royal Highness has no idea what consternation he causes when he suddenly wishes to visit someone without giving them prior notice."

Robbie thought that this was very true in his case.

"I came to ask you for the list of guests, so that my secretary can write out the names to go on the doors."

"I have it here ready for you, my Lord," Francis Knollys replied. "But I have not yet had your choice."

"To tell the truth I have not yet made up my mind. Just tell His Royal Highness that I have a surprise for him and that will keep him happy until I have finally decided who will accompany me."

Francis Knollys laughed and handed Robbie a piece of paper.

"There is no one new," he added. "They are all old friends with whom you have spent many amusing times in the past. I feel sure your party will be a great success."

"Why do you say that?" Robbie asked curiously.

"Because His Royal Highness has never been to your home before. Although he has heard about it and your amazing pictures, it will give him something new and interesting to talk about."

Robbie laughed as he knew only too well that the Prince of Wales was quickly bored with anything which became too familiar. He was always looking for change, excitement and something different – that is what he found when he went from woman to woman.

Thanking Francis Knollys for what he had done for him, Robbie left.

As soon as he was back in his flat, he quickly put the names in an envelope and addressed it to Wenda.

*

When she received his letter on Thursday morning and read the list, Wenda realised just how important they all were.

She only hoped and prayed that they would not be too critical about The Court.

She had done her best.

But never in her father's and mother's time had so many important titled people stayed in her home all at the same time.

It was completely different from having them just for a dinner party and maybe a dance afterwards, but as she already knew they would all arrive on Friday at teatime and not leave until late on Sunday.

She had gone through the menus not once but over and over again with Mrs. Banks and she felt certain that the Prince would enjoy the French dishes they had included.

She realised just how different cooking was for one man to cooking for twelve, all of whom had eaten these special dishes in Paris.

Wenda was only afraid for Robbie's sake that the dishes might not be as delicious as she thought they were and the Prince, if he was not amused this weekend, might not invite him so often to Marlborough House.

Then she told herself that she and Banks had done their very best and if it was not good enough, they could do no more.

Very carefully she wrote the ladies' names on the back of her mother's visiting cards and with some drawing pins she found in the Estate Office she fastened them onto the doors of the bedrooms.

Robbie had also included a rough plan with the list, showing the rooms on the first floor which were to be used by each member of the house party.

The only rooms which did not have a name card were the Master suite and of course Wenda's and she knew that was because no one yet was to be aware that the Prince of Wales was to be Robbie's special guest.

It was a great temptation for her to tell Banks and Mrs. Banks, who would be exceedingly impressed.

But Robbie had told her it was very important that the house party was kept secret just in case the local press were to hear of it.

Wenda had not argued and yet she reckoned that the moment the Prince of Wales appeared there was no doubt that all the servants would recognise him.

They would naturally be wildly excited that he was in their midst and the village would undoubtedly think it the most enthralling thing that had ever happened.

And it was only a question of time before it reached the ears of the gossips of St. Albans where a local paper appeared weekly.

As Robbie had been in such a great hurry to return to London, there was no one to answer her questions or to tell her what more she could do to keep the secret of their most important visitor from being bandied about.

However there was little point in worrying at the moment and she still had a great deal to do.

The Master suite was shining brightly as if it had been rubbed all over with golden sunshine.

Wenda had galvanised Donson into working so hard that he had made the garden look, she thought, almost as beautiful as in the days when they had eight gardeners.

He had also managed to repair the ancient fountain that stood in the centre of the lawn and Wenda clapped her hands with delight when, after lying broken and neglected ever since she could remember, it now threw strong jets of water up into the sky.

She surmised that it was a blessing in disguise that Donson had fallen out with Mr. Hatton and she had paid him herself to work in the garden.

Wenda told him that she would need every flower he could possibly grow, beg, borrow or steal on Friday morning.

"I'll be sure to get all them flowers for you, Miss Wenda," he promised, "don't you a-worry."

"I am not worrying, Donson, because I can rely on you to keep your word. You told me you would make the garden look like new and that is just what you have done!"

Donson was obviously delighted at her praise and she thought that if in the future she had to sell more than one brooch, she would definitely keep him on however extravagant it might seem.

Because she was apprehensive of what Robbie had done in taking away the two entailed pictures, she tried not to think about it.

Fortunately the two empty spaces in the galleries were not obvious and she was convinced that no one who was coming at the weekend would notice them.

Equally she shivered when she thought how angry the Trustees would be if they discovered the truth.

*

Back in London Robbie was also thinking about the pictures as Mr. Hudson had prophesised he would receive even more money than he expected.

He had gone to bed with this thought in his mind on Wednesday night having dined once again with Josofine at the same restaurant in Shepherd's Market.

They had drunk champagne to celebrate the happy day they had spent and Robbie looked a little questioningly at the bill.

He thought how much more expensive it was than when he usually ate there, but how could he give Josofine anything but the best?

It was then he told himself *he had fallen in love*.

He had known it from the first night they had dined together and now he was aware that every moment of the day he found himself becoming more and more enraptured with Josofine.

When she gave him a shy little smile, he felt his heart turn over in his breast and it was something that had not happened to him for a very long time.

Of course Robbie had thought himself attracted and almost in love with the beautiful women he had visited in their husbands' absence or whoever he was paired off with on the secret weekends with the Prince of Wales.

But what he felt then was not what he felt now.

He found himself totally entranced by the natural and unassumed excitement in Josofine 's voice and by the way she listened attentively to everything he said.

And by her laughter which was so unaffected that it was sounds he had never heard before.

'I am head over heels in love,' he told himself on Wednesday night.

At the same time if he asked her to marry him, he would require much more than the sums he would obtain from the sale of two pictures.

On Thursday when he went to bed, he knew that if he had every picture at The Court copied in France so that he could spend the money on Josofine, he would do it.

'I cannot lose her, I just cannot!' he told himself fervently and that whatever he needed to do, even if it was criminal, he would do it rather than lose her.

He thought of her as he lay tossing and sleepless in his friend's bed.

He wanted to go next door and take her in his arms and tell her how much he loved her.

But he knew instinctively as he had known all day that she would not understand and he would still have to be so careful not to frighten her off.

She had run away from France and although he had tried without making it too obvious to satisfy the curiosity he felt about her parents, she had not yet told him what he wanted to know.

'I love her, I do love her,' he told himself over and over again.

But that did not answer the questions he found pressing against his lips and he only prevented himself by a tremendous effort from expressing them.

On Thursday they spent a long day exploring parts of London that Robbie had not seen before.

Josofine had also insisted early in the morning on going to Bond Street to buy a dress – it was after Robbie had told her that he was taking her to the country at the weekend to see his home.

"Is it big or small?" she asked him innocently.

"Actually it is very big, but I will tell you frankly I cannot afford to keep it up in the way it should be."

Josofine did not look surprised.

"I thought because you had such a very small place in London you must be poor," she said. "But you are lucky to have a home in the country."

"Very lucky indeed and I know you will admire my pictures. But they are all entailed, if you understand what that means, onto my son, who perhaps I will never be able to afford to have."

"I have heard of entailment," replied Josofine, "and some families have it in France. But of course the French noblemen lost so many of their treasures in the Revolution that their châteaux are not as grand as they used to be."

"I am very anxious for you to see my house, but, as I have said, it is not as fine as it should be, although we are making every effort to make it comfortable for the party I am entertaining at the weekend."

Josofine was silent for a moment and then she said,

"As you are having a party, would it perhaps be better if I stayed in London, hoping that when your guests have gone, you will return and look after me again."

"Is that what you want?" Robbie asked her.

"No, of course not. I don't want to lose you, but I would find it very exciting to see your home."

There was silence while Robbie thought it would be fantastic for him to take her there.

He could imagine her looking exquisitely lovely against the pictures in the galleries.

And he was quite certain she would look even more beautiful than the Madonnas and the Goddesses depicted by the great Masters.

Because he was silent Josofine remarked quickly,

"I will stay here if you want me to."

"I want you to see Creswell Court," Robbie replied, "and you know that I have no wish to leave you alone in London. I would feel very worried if I did so."

"You were quite right in telling me that I should not have come to London alone, but I cannot presume on you for ever, Robbie."

He just gazed at her.

He wondered how he could put into words how impossible it was for him to lose her.

'I want her! I want her!' every nerve in his body cried out.

Yet commonsense told him that he could not afford a wife. What sort of life would she have with him unless he went on illegally taking down his pictures and sending them over to France.

"I don't know what you are thinking, but it's really worrying you," Josofine said unexpectedly.

"I am worrying about you. It is something we will talk about when the weekend is over."

Josephine smiled at him.

"You are quite certain you want me to come?"

"Of course I want you," he answered, "and if you don't come with me I shall stay in London and my guests will have to look after themselves."

Josofine chuckled.

"Now you are being ridiculous. Think how angry your guests would be if their host was not present to pay them compliments and to make quite certain they enjoyed themselves.

"Very well, we *will* enjoy ourselves and only when the party has gone will we talk about your future."

He knew as he spoke it was an issue she wanted to avoid. She had still not confided in him who she was or who the man was she had run away from.

She had however removed the wedding ring from her finger and Robbie was now aware that he would have to tell her to put it back.

It was impossible for him to produce a young girl at His Royal Highness's parties. It had always been married ladies who had been there in the past.

The Prince was convinced that all young girls were dangerous in that they talked too much among themselves.

At each secret house party he had enjoyed with His Royal Highness there had never been any question of the ladies not being married.

"We must depart early for the country on Friday morning," Robbie told Josofine . "There will be such a lot for me to see to before my guests arrive. So I would like to leave London soon after ten o'clock."

"I will be ready," replied Josofine. "But if I am going to the country, I would like to go back to that nice shop we visited in Bond Street and buy myself one more dress to wear and perhaps another evening gown."

It was with difficulty that Robbie prevented himself from asking her how she could afford it.

However he took her there before they started off again on another tour of London and he waited outside in the carriage he had hired for the day.

While Josephine was in the shop, he found himself thinking again and again how much he was in love.

How entrancing Josofine was.

He had never before felt anything quite so thrilling or glorious and he knew that if he lost her he would never again feel the same as he did now.

'I love her, I adore her,' he whispered to himself.

He found it almost impossible not to run into the shop just to see if she was still there.

Because she was out shopping and women were the same all the world over, she took longer than he expected.

At last she came out with two large dress-boxes which were put down on the floor of the carriage.

"I thought you must be buying up the whole shop," he commented ruefully.

"I am sorry if I was a long time. I had to try them on and the first two were too big for me."

"I am absolutely convinced you would look lovely in anything you wore," Robbie sighed. "Therefore it was sheer extravagance for you to buy a new dress."

"I really want to look pretty for your friends and of course *you*."

"It would be just impossible for you to be anything else, Josofine."

As the carriage was moving off he thought it was a mistake at this moment to go on talking about themselves.

He still could not understand how she managed to buy goods from the shop which he knew was an extremely expensive one, and he found it hard to believe that when she was running away she had brought a large amount of money with her and yet she must have done so.

He was only worried if it would last her very much longer.

They spent the rest of the day visiting museums and looking at the outside of Buckingham Palace.

They also drove to the docks because she had read about them and wanted to know if they were exactly as they were described.

All Robbie wanted to do was to make her happy.

So later in the evening he took her to Drury Lane and they watched the dancers who had entranced London and a great many gentlemen like himself.

Afterwards they went to dine at another quiet but attractive restaurant where Robbie had often been before.

They were shown into a comfortable alcove where those who occupied them could see rather than be seen and regardless of the expense Robbie ordered the best dishes and the best wines.

He thought as he looked at Josofine that although he had often dined here with the most acclaimed beauties in London, she was lovelier in every way than they were.

Yet what did seem extraordinary to him was that while they had talked on so many divergent subjects, he still knew no more about her.

Each time he asked Josephine a leading question she somehow managed to avoid it.

He told himself now that after the weekend she would have to be open and then she must tell him more about herself.

He could not go on as they were at the moment and yet he knew that in some extraordinary way he was happier than he had ever been in his whole life.

'I love you, I adore you,' he wanted to tell Josofine, but he was still afraid of frightening her away.

He not only wanted to protect her from everyone else but also from himself.

'If I scare her,' he thought, 'she might disappear as quickly as she appeared. Then what would I do?'

He could all too clearly imagine himself searching France to find her – probably being unsuccessful, so that she would be lost to him for ever.

"Why are you looking worried?" Josofine asked.

"I did not know I was, but all the same I do worry about you and what will happen to you in the future."

"I am so content with the present that I only think of what we are doing at this particular moment not what will happen tomorrow."

"I wish I could feel like that too, but I cannot help wondering what we will do when the weekend ends. Will you want to come back to London or would you like to stay in the country?"

He thought she would give him a straight answer, but she simply responded,

"Why should we worry about tomorrow when we have still a little of today left, Robbie? It was so kind of you to take me to Drury Lane and I am enjoying being here in this charming restaurant with such delicious food."

"I have enjoyed it too and I am looking forward to tomorrow when I will show you my home. But I will have to think of where I can take you on Monday."

There was a little pause and then Josofine sighed,

"Let's wait until Monday comes."

She looked at Robbie imploringly and because he thought that every word she said was like music and every movement she made was elegance itself, he found himself saying weakly,

"All right, let us enjoy today or rather tonight and forget all our difficulties until Monday."

"Of course it is the right answer to your question," Josofine added approvingly. "And it will spoil tomorrow and the next two days if we keep thinking of what will happen in the future. I want to enjoy the moment when I see your home and all the lovely things you have told me you have in it."

It was so much easier, Robbie decided, to listen to her than to go on worrying.

But he still wanted frantically and persistently to learn the truth about her.

Then he could look ahead into the future and, if he was honest with himself, decide if he could ask Josofine to marry him.

He had made up his mind a long time ago that it would be impossible for him to marry anyone unless by some miracle he found a way of making enough money to live at Creswell Court as his parents had done.

He wanted to improve the estate until it brought in the income it had in the past and even to think of it made the problem seem daunting and hopelessly difficult.

So he had put it on one side and enjoyed himself in exactly same way as the Prince of Wales had with every beautiful woman he was attracted to.

Yet now he was in love as he had never been in love before.

He wanted to be married.

He wanted a family.

To be truthful he wanted just an ordinary life with the woman he loved.

It had never happened to him before and he had thought he would always be amused with the endless balls, the dinner parties, the weekends –

Yet now it seemed absolutely incredible that one young woman, about whom he knew absolutely nothing, should change his whole life.

She had appeared from across the English Channel, and everything he had thought of as desirable was now of no significance beside her.

'I want to be with her. I want her love and I want her to be mine.'

The words kept repeating themselves in his mind as he looked at Josofine across the table.

He knew he was frightened, as he had never been frightened before, that he might lose her.

Perhaps if he did not attract her enough, she might suddenly decide to go back to France.

They sat talking until they were the last people in the restaurant and then they drove back in a hired hansom cab to Mount Street.

Robbie did not attempt to touch her as they drove along Piccadilly and yet he was acutely aware of her beside him.

He could smell the sweet scent that came from her body every time she moved.

They entered his lodgings, said goodnight to the porter at the door and climbed up the stairs.

Josofine handed him the key of his flat door and he opened it.

The curtains had not been drawn and the moonlight was coming in through the windows turning the carpet to silver.

Through the open door Robbie could see the lamp which stood by his bed, and it must have been lit before Josofine went out and although it was turned low the room seemed warm and golden.

Josofine moved to the window to look down at the moonlit street below.

"It has been a lovely evening," she sighed. "I do not think I have ever been so happy."

"Nor have I," Robbie replied.

"Is that true?" she quizzed.

"Of course it is true. Surely you understand that when I am with you I am happier than I have ever been."

Josephine looked at him and he realised that her blue eyes were searching his face – she wanted to be quite sure that he was telling her the truth.

Very slowly, as if he was afraid to do so, he put his arms round her.

"I love you, Josofine," he whispered. "I love you, my darling, with all my heart and soul. There is no one else in the whole world for me except you."

He felt the little quiver that went through her and then he drew her closer to him and his lips were on hers.

It was a very gentle kiss.

A kiss almost of reverence.

As he felt the softness and innocence of her lips, he knew instinctively it was the first time she had ever been kissed.

He drew her even closer to him.

Never in his life had a kiss been so wonderful or aroused in him strange feelings he had never known.

Then because he was still afraid of scaring her, he raised his head and almost instinctively she moved a little away from him.

"I love you," he repeated. "I love you, and there are no words to tell you how much you mean to me."

Then with a superhuman effort he walked towards the door.

As he reached it he turned back and said in a voice that did not sound like his own,

"Sleep peacefully, my darling, and remember I love you."

He closed the door and walked slowly down the passage to his friend's flat.

CHAPTER FIVE

They started off at ten o'clock the next morning.

Robbie felt that no one could look more attractive than Josofine.

She was wearing what he reckoned she must have bought yesterday. It was a country dress, rather plain but which seemed to accentuate her beauty. To match it she sported a very pretty straw hat that allowed her dark hair to curl against her pink and white cheeks.

As the sun was shining and the birds were singing it was the perfect day to be going to the country.

Robbie had risen early and gone to see the manager of the stables where he hired a post-chaise.

And he had agreed with the manager that he should drive two new horses that were fresh and young without having to take a groom with him.

"I know I can trust you, my Lord," he said, "to look after me horses properly."

"I promise you they will have the best food and the most comfortable accommodation," replied Robbie stoutly.

The manager laughed.

"That's more than a lot of us gets these days!"

Robbie agreed with him and he was thinking of his small flat and the difficulty he had in paying the rent.

He calculated that he and Josofine should arrive shortly after luncheon at Creswell Court.

He was certain Wenda would be off her head seeing to everything in the house.

He knew there was a good posting inn about five miles from his home and he had occasionally visited it over the years.

They had not gone far before Josofine commented,

"I can see you are a very good driver, Robbie."

He smiled at her.

"I enjoy driving, but most of all riding."

It suddenly struck him that he had never asked her if she could ride and before he could do so, she admitted,

"I enjoy riding too. I have two horses of my own in France and I love both of them."

"Has your father a large stable?" Robbie enquired.

There was a pause before Josofine answered,

"Do tell me about your horses. How old were you when you rode for the first time?"

She was being evasive again, but Robbie sensed it would be foolish to spoil the day by pressing her to tell him what she did not want him to know.

They did not talk much on the way as Robbie was concentrating on giving the horses their heads. They were certainly faster than any he had driven from that stable.

They reached the posting inn just a little before one o'clock and as he turned into the yard, Robbie told her,

"We are having luncheon here. They will be so busy at home preparing for this evening that I don't want to bother them for an extra meal."

"That is kind and considerate of you," Josofine said softly. "I have noticed since I first met you that unlike other men you are always thinking of other people."

"Perhaps you have met the wrong sort of men – "

He saw as he spoke that she gave a little shiver.

She was obviously thinking again of the man she had run away from.

Robbie was determined at luncheon to prevent her from thinking about anything that made her unhappy and so he told her stories of his childhood – of his first pony and his first ride out hunting and how much he would love to own a racing stable.

She listened most attentively to everything he was saying, but told him nothing about her own childhood.

When they set off again it was after two o'clock and Robbie wondered if Wenda had expected him earlier.

Perhaps she had plenty of dire problems for him to solve at the last moment.

He did not speak of his fears to Josofine and only as they drew nearer to The Court did he venture,

"I think I must explain to you that although I own a very big house with magnificent pictures in it, I really have no money. Today you will see it as it was when my father and mother were alive and how I would always like it to be."

He realised that when Josofine was listening, her head turned towards him.

"But I am being quite frank with you," he went on, "when I say this is a special party and it is very different from the way I live ordinarily."

Josofine had kept her big blue eyes fixed on him and he knew she was absorbing every word he spoke.

Looking ahead he added,

"What I am really saying in rather a roundabout way is that if you will marry me and make me the happiest man in the world, we will have the house and the grounds but not enough money to keep it as you will see it now."

Josofine made a little murmur, but before she could speak he continued,

"I am not asking you to give me a decision now. But I want to spend this weekend believing I will not lose you and that you will be mine for ever."

He drew in his breath before he finished,

"But it would be wrong to deceive you and let you think that it would be all plain sailing."

They reached a pair of impressive iron gates that were much in need of repair.

He turned up the drive with its great oak trees on either side and then ahead Josofine had her first sight of Creswell Court with the bright sun glittering on a hundred windows and turning the Elizabethan bricks pink. It was breathtakingly lovely.

She gave a little cry of sheer delight.

"Is that really your home?" she asked. "Oh, how lucky you are!"

"That is what I have always thought myself until finance became so difficult."

He did not speak again until they drew up outside the house and as they did so a man who Robbie thought vaguely he had seen before in the village came hurrying to the horses' heads.

"Afternoon, my Lord," he said cheerily as Robbie climbed down. "I be told to be lookin' out for you and I'll see to the horses."

Robbie thought it typical of Wenda to remember that he would require someone to look after the horses.

He and Josofine walked up the steps and into the hall.

It was Robbie who gave a gasp of astonishment.

There were three footmen, who he had never seen before wearing the family livery.

In the hall itself the pictures, the grandfather clock, the mantelpiece and the stairs were all shining.

It looked incredibly unlike the drab dusty old place where just a few days ago he had said goodbye to his sister.

Before he could say anything, Banks came hurrying from beneath the stairs. He was looking not only smarter than Robbie had seen him for many years now but in some strange way younger.

"It's so good to see you, my Lord, and everything's prepared as your Lordship wanted. If you'll go into the drawing room, I'll tell Mrs. Stevenson you're here. I think madam would like to tidy herself after the long drive."

Robbie realised that Banks was saying exactly what Wenda had told him to say.

"That is most kind of you, Banks, and perhaps a footman would take Madame Frazer's luggage out of the back of the carriage."

Banks snapped his fingers and one of the footmen hurried out of the front door and down the steps.

"Come with me into the drawing room," Robbie invited Josofine.

Banks opened the door for them.

Once again Robbie gasped and found it difficult not to cry out with amazement at the transformation before his eyes.

Because he and Wenda never sat in this room, it always seemed drab and dreary and now everything was glittering.

The pictures were all by famous French artists and they seemed to catch the sunshine as it poured through the windows and reflected into the room.

There was a profusion of flowers and the china on the mantelpiece and on the tables was sparkling as it never had before.

"Oh, what a pretty room!" exclaimed Josofine.

"That is just what I was thinking myself!"

As he spoke, Mrs. Stevenson, dressed as she used to be long ago in rustling black silk, appeared at the door and Robbie noticed with a smile that she even had her silver chatelaine at her waist.

"Good afternoon, my Lord," she intoned. "We're all very glad to see you here and I hope you had a pleasant journey."

"We did indeed and now if you will take madam to her bedroom, I have a few things to look to before my guests arrive."

Mrs. Stevenson gave him a smile and nodded.

He knew she was aware that Wenda was in hiding and the guests would not know that she was in the house.

Josofine joined Mrs. Stevenson and as they started to walk back into the hall, the housekeeper said to him,

"You'll find someone waiting to see you, my Lord, in the West gallery."

"Thank you," Robbie replied and before Josofine put her foot on the stairs he had started to run down the corridors which led to the gallery.

As Mrs. Stevenson had indicated, Wenda was there waiting for him, giving the last finishing touch to one of the pictures.

As he walked into the gallery, Wenda put down her duster and with a cry of joy she ran towards him.

"You are here! Oh, Robbie I am so pleased to see you."

She flung herself against him and he kissed both her cheeks before he said,

"You are either a magician or a witch, Wenda. If you had lived in the Middle Ages, they would have burnt you at the stake! I have never ever seen such a marvellous rebirth as you have achieved in this house."

"You have not seen it all yet," purred Wenda, "and if only we had had a little more time we could have done better."

Robbie put up his hands.

"I know, I know, but it is absolutely astounding. I could not believe my eyes when I saw those footmen in the hall!"

"There are four of them and I think they will all be very good, but Robbie, I have so much to tell you and I do suppose you have someone with you."

"Yes, of course, and she is with Mrs. Stevenson at the moment, so tell me first if I can help in any way."

"I am just hoping I have not forgotten anything, but Banks has been a tower of strength as you might imagine. Mrs. Banks is a bit fluttery, but I feel sure you will find tonight's dinner delicious."

"All I can say, Wenda, is thank you, *thank you*."

"Don't thank me too soon. Something may well go wrong at the last moment. By the way no one knows yet who your special guest is."

"That is just what I was going to ask you and it is clever of you to have kept it a secret."

"I was tempted to tell the Bankses, but they will all be thrilled later tonight because however secret the Prince intends it to be, you know just as well as I do they will all recognise him."

"Of course they will, but once he is behind closed doors it will be hard for anyone to suspect he is here until the weekend is nearly over."

He then looked intently round the gallery and all the pictures had been cleaned and the parquet flooring was bright with polish.

"You really have been brilliant. How many people did it take to do all this, Wenda?"

"I have not dared to count them all, Robbie. But I think in the end nearly everyone in the village has given a hand one way or another.

"And by the way there are four men in the stables and Mr. Wentworth has been simply marvellous about the Racecourse."

"Surely we cannot ride on it in any comfort. I was hoping His Royal Highness would have forgotten about it, although he did mention it when he suggested he came here as a guest."

"You told me that was what he wanted," Wenda said. "If you recall, Mr. Wentworth had some connection with the Grand National."

"Yes, of course."

"Well he retired to the next village to us. So I went to see him and almost on my knees asked for his help."

"And he actually agreed to help?"

"He was delighted to do so, because I think he is bored having nothing to do now he is over seventy."

"He can hardly have restored the Racecourse in a few days."

"He said it was impossible, but with the aid of half-a-dozen men they have put up some new jumps."

"*Jumps!*" cried Robbie.

"I am sure it would amuse His Royal Highness to watch his friends racing over the jumps even though the ground is not particularly even."

Robbie put his arms round his sister's shoulders.

"All I can say, Wenda, is that you are a genius and you should not be wasting your talent here in the country."

"I must admit I was frightened we might not be in time for you, but I have never enjoyed myself more. I felt I was a General giving orders to a very large Army!"

Robbie laughed because he could not help it.

"You are such a clever girl and I only regret that you will not hear the compliments His Royal Highness and his friends will pay you even though you are anonymous."

"At least the house looks fairly respectable, but if you had given me a bit longer I could have done marvels."

"I am not complaining about the miracle you have performed. I am only telling you, Wenda, I think you are magnificent and it is most unfair that you cannot come into dinner so we can all toast you."

Wenda laughed.

"I will be very busy in the kitchen with my sleeves rolled up making the French dishes Papa always enjoyed."

"And I will certainly enjoy them too if only because you have made it all possible."

Robbie kissed her cheek and declared,

"I have so much to tell you when there is time. But for goodness sake keep out of sight otherwise the guests will be inconveniently curious about you."

"They are not likely to go into the kitchen or the scullery and if they did, they would hardly expect to find your sister and chatelaine of Cresswell Court on her knees scrubbing the floor!"

"Oh, for goodness sake, Wenda, I hope you have found someone to do that!"

"Of course I did. I am only teasing you. In fact I myself have concentrated on the pictures and they really do look different."

"They do indeed," Robbie agreed, "and I am going to take the lady I brought with me round the house before the rest of the party arrive."

"Don't show her the kitchen, because that is where I will be and I'm sure if she is French, as you told me when you sent me the guest list, that she will fully appreciate the Fragonards and the Bouchers if none of the others."

"She will enjoy them all, I am sure."

He wanted to tell Wenda how much Josofine meant to him. But he thought it would be a mistake at this stage.

Wenda picked up her polish and took off her apron, which was already smeared from working on the picture frames.

Because he was afraid Josofine might be looking for him, Robbie hurried back the way he had come.

He found as he had expected that she had taken off her hat, tidied her hair and was in the drawing room.

"I have been waiting for you," she said, "and please show me your pictures before the others arrive. If they are as beautiful as the ones here, they must be fantastic."

"That is what I hope you will think, so come along with me, Josephine."

He took her first to the East gallery just in case they should bump into Wenda coming away from the West gallery.

The East gallery had been cleaned up the same as the West gallery.

He showed her first a picture he thought was one of the best at The Court and his father had always said one of the most valuable in the whole collection.

It was '*The Mystical Marriage of Saint Catherine of Alexandria*' painted by Hans Memling.

Robbie always thought that it was most attractive and yet when he looked at it now he saw that Josofine was far more beautiful than Saint Catherine.

She was thrilled with the painting and as he took her round the East Gallery, she shuddered at the macabre '*Portrait of a Man*' by Antonello da Messina and stunned by Raphael's picture of '*Saint George and the Dragon*'.

"How can you be so lucky?" she asked, "to own all these beautiful pictures, Robbie?"

"As I have explained, it is only for my lifetime."

"They are so beautiful," enthused Josofine.

"But not as beautiful as you – "

She looked at him and it was impossible for either of them to look away.

Slowly he put out his arms, then pulled Josofine gently towards him.

"I love you," he told her, "and you are so lovely. There is no picture of a woman or a Goddess in the whole wide world as exquisite as you."

"That is what I want you to think," she whispered.

Then he was kissing her.

Kissing her at first gently then more demandingly, as if he was afraid of losing her.

How long they stood there in the gallery Robbie had no idea.

Suddenly there was the sound of someone running along the passage.

As they moved apart one of the new footmen burst in through the door.

"Mr. Banks says will you come at once, my Lord?" he gasped breathlessly, "because your guests be arrivin'."

"I am coming right now," Robbie replied.

He took hold of Josofine by the hand and drew her out into the passage.

It was not long after three o'clock and it surprised him that any of the party should turn up so early.

And then he saw Banks rushing out of the drawing room and there was an expression on his face of agitation, at the same time of excitement and it told Robbie who it was who had come so early.

There was no need for Banks to say anything. He just opened the drawing room door.

As Robbie ventured in still holding Josofine by the hand, he saw the Prince of Wales standing in front of the fireplace looking at a picture by Boucher.

Seated in one of the armchairs and looking very elegant was the Duchess of Manchester.

Releasing Josofine's hand Robbie walked quickly across the room and he had almost reached the Prince of Wales before he turned round.

"I welcome Your Royal Highness to my home," he breathed, "and I apologise for not being on the doorstep, but I did not expect Your Royal Highness quite so early."

"I would like to see your pictures before the other guests arrive," the Prince of Wales replied. "And I am already entranced with this Boucher which I would like to possess myself."

"It delights me to hear you say so, sir."

Then he turned back as Josofine had just reached him.

"May I present Madame – "

Before he could actually say her name to his sheer astonishment he heard the Prince exclaim,

"Josofine! What are you doing here?"

"*Mon Parrain, mon cher Parrain*!" Josofine cried. "I did not expect you and it is wonderful to see you!"

As she spoke she almost threw herself against the Prince and he kissed her on both cheeks.

Robbie stared at them in amazement.

Josofine had spoken in French and Robbie knew that *Parrain* meant Godfather.

Then he asked himself how could she possibly be the Goddaughter of the Prince of Wales?

"I did not know you were in England," the Prince was saying. "Why did your father not notify me?"

"I am here," Josofine replied, "because I have run away. Oh, dear, my wonderful *Parrain*, please help me. I wanted to ask you to do so, but was too frightened in case you sent me home."

If Robbie was now looking astonished, so was the Prince of Wales.

Josofine was looking up at him beseechingly and he took her arm and sitting on the sofa pulled her down beside him.

"Now start at the beginning," he said, "and tell me exactly what is happening and why you are here."

Before Josofine could speak, the Duchess, as if she felt she was being neglected, rose from her chair.

"As I can see I am not wanted," she said, "I think I will go up and rest a little after the journey. It was quite a long drive from London and I really am a little tired."

"Of course, of course, if that is what you must do," the Prince of Wales blustered, but he was still gazing at Josofine.

"Forgive me, please" Robbie came in quickly, "for not greeting you as I should, but I was astonished that the lady with me is already known to His Royal Highness."

"That is obvious," sniffed the Duchess.

They walked towards the door and Robbie opened it. To his relief he saw Banks standing outside and with him was Mrs. Stevenson.

"Oh, this is my housekeeper, Your Grace," he said to the Duchess. "Do allow her to take you upstairs to your room and when you have rested I want to show you some of my pictures that I believe could rival those in your own beautiful houses."

The Duchess smiled at him and because she was really a charming and sweet person, she responded,

"I should love to when all the drama is over."

They both laughed and then she walked away with Mrs. Stevenson and Robbie hurried back into the drawing room.

He had missed the start of Josofine's conversation with His Royal Highness, but as he joined them she was saying,

"Papa was determined I should marry him simply because he and Mama thought it very smart for me to be a reigning Princess. But I hated him from the first moment I saw him – "

"I can very easily understand that, my dear," the Prince of Wales remarked soothingly.

Robbie sat down pulling up a chair near to them.

"You are now hearing all the secrets, Your Royal Highness, that have been kept from me. I only know that Josofine is now pretending to be a married woman and she arrived alone in London knowing no one."

"Why on earth did you not come to *me*," the Prince of Wales asked Josofine. "You know I would have been delighted for you to stay with me at Marlborough House."

"I was scared that you would think Papa was right and that I should marry that dreadful Prince."

"What Prince?" Robbie asked because he could not prevent himself.

"Prince Frederick of Gurenburg," Josofine replied.

"A fella I've always disliked," the Prince of Wales came back sharply. "And, of course, Josofine was quite right. He would be only marrying her for her money."

"*Her money!*" Robbie exclaimed as if he could not help it.

The Prince looked at him almost rebukingly.

"You must have known that Josofine's mother had an American mother, who was an heiress in her own right and was given an annual income of forty thousand pounds a year by the Emperor Napoleon III when she was married to Antoine de Noailles, Duc de Mouchy."

"I had no idea of that," Robbie stammered.

Even as he spoke he was aware that he had met the Duc and Duchesse de Mouchy when they were staying at Marlborough House and he had learnt then that they were extremely rich.

Now he recognised that Josofine, being their only child, would inherit a huge fortune.

Prince Frederick, who ruled a small Principality in North Germany, was doubtless looking for an heiress to share his throne.

"So you ran away," the Prince of Wales was saying. "I think you should have come to me immediately you set foot in London."

"It is just what I thought I might do, Your Royal Highness, and I knew that you would be kind and would understand why I ran away. At the same time, because you are such friends with my Papa and Mama, you might have insisted that I went back to them."

"How did you meet this young man?" he asked, looking at Robbie.

"He came aboard the yacht I had travelled on when I was wondering where I might find a hotel. The man who had brought me across the Channel asked him to look after me which he has done very very kindly."

"I am not surprised," the Prince of Wales said with a smile at Robbie, who now piped up,

"What we want, sir, is to be married immediately, before Josofine's father and mother decide that I am not good enough for her. I cannot offer her a throne, only this house, which in fact I cannot afford to keep up in the way Your Royal Highness is seeing it now."

He knew as he spoke that the Prince was listening and there was an expression on his face he recognised only too well. If there was one thing His Royal Highness really enjoyed it was being given a puzzle or a difficult problem to solve.

It was what he had always wanted to do with the affairs of the nation, but the Queen resolutely refused to give him even the smallest part to play.

"Please, *mon Parrain*, please," Josofine was saying, "please help us or I will find myself married to that horrid German Prince and you know how gloomy those German Palaces can be."

Robbie knew this was true. He had visited two German Principalities with the Prince of Wales and found them appallingly dull. After the second one the Prince had said firmly he was not accepting another invitation there.

Robbie well knew that the French, like the Duc de Mouchy, were very ambitious for their children and the Duc would be really delighted at the idea of his beautiful daughter becoming Her Royal Highness.

Now Josofine was holding tightly onto the Prince of Wales's hand and looking up at him pleadingly.

"Help us, *please* help us," she repeated.

The Prince smiled.

"I suppose, Robbie, you have a Chapel here."

"Actually it's the Church in the Park, a very old one and badly in need of repair. I pay the Parson a stipend and he's a charming old man who was very fond of both my parents."

"Excellent! Tell him you'll be married on Sunday and *I* will be giving away the bride."

Josofine gave a cry of delight and she put her arms round the Prince's neck and kissed him.

"I knew you would help us! I knew you would! Oh, *mon cher Parrain*, could anyone else in the world have such a wonderful and generous Godfather?"

Robbie did not speak for a moment and then he asked hesitantly,

"There is only one point, sir, would it be legal if Josofine is a Catholic?"

To his surprise the Prince of Wales laughed.

"My dear boy, I am not as stupid as all that. Of course, if she was a Catholic she could not marry you as I am now arranging."

Robbie looked bewildered and the Prince of Wales went on,

"She has not told you – indeed she may not have remembered the fact – she was born rather prematurely at Sandringham and, as there was some fear that she might not live, she was baptised by my Private Chaplain there, and I became her Godfather."

Robbie gave a gasp, but did not speak as the Prince added,

"Afterwards when her family returned to France, she was, I understand, baptised again because her father is a Catholic."

Robbie gave a deep sigh of relief.

"I will send someone down to the Vicarage now to tell the Vicar you wish to speak to him. I am sure Your Royal Highness will convince him better than I can that I do not need a Special Marriage Licence."

"Of course there will be no difficulty about that," the Prince retorted.

If Robbie had tried to arrange a special amusement to entertain the Prince, he could not have succeeded better than by giving him a problem to solve and a battle to fight.

He was absolutely delighted at the idea of stealing a march on the Duc de Mouchy even though he was a friend.

He knew that if he gave his blessing to the marriage between Lord Creswell and Josofine, who, as the daughter of a French Duc, had the rank of Comtesse, it would be impossible for her father to make any difficulties about it afterwards.

"Everything will be fine, my boy," the Prince said to Robbie, "and all we have to decide now is whether you, Josofine, or I should break the news to her parents."

"I know the answer to that, sir," Robbie answered and the Prince of Wales chuckled.

As the other guests arrived there was no question of Josofine being introduced as Madame Frazer.

The Prince told the story of how she had run away and everyone found it very romantic and exciting.

"It was incredibly brave of you," the Duchess of Manchester sighed, "to arrive in London knowing no one and having nowhere to go."

"I just knew I would be welcome at my Godfather's house, but I was so afraid he would think it right for me to marry the Prince because he had a throne."

There was no doubt that night despite the fact that, although the other ladies were great beauties in their own right, Josofine was the star.

There was no need for her to wear any sparkling jewellery or an elaborate gown as her eyes were shining.

She was so happy and thrilled that everyone else felt themselves elated too.

They drank her and Robbie's health at dinner and no one was surprised when as the long and delicious meal came to an end Robbie and Josofine disappeared.

They sat talking in the drawing room too intrigued by what had happened even to look at the bridge tables.

It was the Duchess who sighed rather wistfully,

"They are both so young and so happy it makes me feel as if I too was eighteen again!

"That is exactly what you look now," the Prince flattered her. "And I am sure you are more beautiful now than you were when you first emerged upon the Social world."

Because the Duchess was a German by birth, they were careful not to be too rude about Prince Frederick and Robbie learned that not only the Prince of Wales had no liking for him, but neither had any of the other gentlemen.

When Robbie took Josofine away, he asked her,

"Why did you not trust me? Why did you not tell me?"

"Because after you had been so kind to me the first night and let me stay in your flat," she answered, "I was afraid of losing you."

"Losing me!" Robbie exclaimed.

"I thought at first I would tell you about the Prince and ask you if I would be wise to go to see my Godfather – then it was just so wonderful being with you."

She said the last words shyly and Robbie put his arms round her.

"I loved you and adored you from the first moment I set eyes on you. Now I cannot believe it is real we are to be married and you will be mine for ever."

"And we will live here in this beautiful house and everyone I know will envy us. Not because we have all those magnificent pictures, but because we are *so* happy.

There was nothing Robbie could say in words.

He could only draw her close into his arms and kiss her until they both felt they were flying into the sky.

"I love you, Josofine. I adore you," he repeated over and over.

Eventually some time later he then forced himself to take Josofine back so that he could look after his guests.

As they went into the drawing room, the happiness on their faces made everyone there a little envious.

The two of them seemed to light up the room with their love.

CHAPTER SIX

Wenda had taken a great deal of trouble with Mrs. Banks over the dinner. She had some difficulty in making the dishes which Robbie had told her the Prince of Wales really enjoyed,

"He loves caviar and orteians," he had said.

Wenda had made a hopeless gesture with her hands.

"We are not likely to find them here in the country!"

"No, I know, but you might be able to find some oysters. His Royal Highness always says his ideal supper dish is grilled oysters."

"I will try," Wenda promised, but she was not very optimistic.

She had remembered that Robbie said his favourite way of cooking pheasant was to have it served stuffed with a woodcock which in its turn was stuffed with truffles.

It was the wrong time of year for pheasant, but she thought a peahen with a teal inside and served on a golden platter would be almost as good. She and Mrs. Banks had added truffles and the delicious sauce her father had loved.

She felt sure that His Royal Highness would not be disappointed.

They had also made him a very special pudding of fresh strawberries and ice-cream in a meringue basket.

Wenda had decorated every dish either with fruit or herbs and they looked very pretty when they were carried into the dining room.

She was feeling quite exhausted when dinner at last was coming to an end.

Very quietly she opened the door that led up to the large minstrels' gallery overlooking the dining room and standing still at the back, she knew that no one would hear or see her.

The table was decorated with flowers and Banks had fished out of the safe the finest silver ornaments that Wenda had not seen since she was a child. The George III candlesticks were on the table and the whole room was gleaming.

But what really interested her were the guests.

As she had not been allowed to meet them, she had to guess who each one was.

The Prince of Wales was exactly as he looked in the portraits she had seen in magazines and newspapers. It would have been impossible to think he was anyone else.

The ladies were all looking exceedingly glamorous especially as all but one of them were wearing diamonds in their hair – not the large tiaras which Wenda knew they would wear on formal occasions, but small delicate ones.

On one lady, who Wenda felt must be the Duchess of Manchester, it was made of small diamond flowers with green leaves which she supposed were emeralds.

She had tried to remember while writing out their names what they had looked like in the portraits she had seen in magazines.

Wenda was wondering who was on the Prince of Wales's left and she supposed she must be Madame Frazer, who Robbie had brought as his guest.

She was certainly extremely pretty but did not look entirely English and she was much younger than the other ladies.

Robbie was sitting beside her and they kept looking at each other in what seemed a very intimate manner.

It then suddenly struck her with unease that Robbie might fall in love and want to marry someone.

He had never hinted at it in the past, but it would perhaps mean she would have to leave The Court and find somewhere else to live – then she told herself he could not afford a wife and there was no need for her to worry about that eventuality.

Everyone seemed to be enjoying themselves and the Prince of Wales was laughing heartily at some of the jokes although she could not hear them.

Finally tired because she had been working so hard, she walked wearily upstairs.

Wenda's was the only room without a name on the door and she went in thinking how quiet and peaceful it was after all the hurly-burly in the kitchen.

She undressed, climbed into bed and blew out the oil lamp on the table.

Then she realised she was not as tired as she had thought. She had brought with her from the library a book on all the Kings and Queens of England that she found fascinating.

'I will read for a little while,' she decided. 'They will make a noise when they come upstairs and wake me anyway.'

She lit three candles near her bed in an attractive holder consisting of four cupids. She had been given it by her parents for her birthday when she was sixteen.

She propped up her pillows and opening the history book began to read, wondering if Robbie would come and say goodnight to her before he went to his room.

It would be so disappointing if she was fast asleep and he could not tell her how much the guests had enjoyed the dinner.

In the drawing room the Prince of Wales played one rubber of bridge and then he said he was going to bed.

"I find it hard to concentrate when there is so much excitement going on," he sighed. "Robbie has told me that tomorrow we are going to take our horses over the new jumps and some of them are very high. So I do think we should not be too late tonight."

He realised as he was speaking that the ladies were giving the men they had arrived with inviting looks from under their eyelashes and the Prince himself was always finding the Duchess most alluring.

They walked upstairs talking loudly and laughing as they went to their own rooms.

No one had noticed, except the Prince, that instead of following them, Robbie and Josofine had disappeared.

He had whispered to her that he wanted her to see the moonlight in the garden and they slipped away without anyone realising they were doing so until they had gone.

At the end of the garden there was a little Wendy House, where Robbie and Wenda had played as children. There was an old and rather dilapidated sofa in it, but it was still quite comfortable.

They passed the pretty fountain which to Robbie's surprise was playing and the moonlight caught the droplets of water as they were flung up into the sky.

The fountain made the garden seem much more enchanted than it had ever been.

As they went into the Wendy House Robbie took Josofine in his arms and his lips found hers and then they could only think of each other.

Wenda had only read a little of her book when she heard the guests coming up the stairs. They all seemed to be laughing and talking at the same time.

But she did not miss the Prince's deep voice and the musical laughter of the ladies.

She thought how smart and elegant they had looked in the dining room and she wondered if the day would ever come when she would be hostess as her mother had been, sitting at the end of the table with the most distinguished male guests on either side of her and Robbie at the top.

Then she told herself she was only dreaming.

It was very unlikely that anything as glamorous as tonight would ever happen again at The Court.

She felt sure that Robbie would be tempted to sell more of the pictures after this weekend, but it was too dangerous and somehow, though she was not quite certain how, she must dissuade him from doing so.

In the passage outside she heard the doors closing one after another and she was surprised that they did not linger longer.

'Perhaps Robbie will come and see me now,' she mused.

She still had no idea why the party was so secret or why each gentleman brought a special lady guest with him.

She just believed it was another way of amusing the Prince of Wales or allowing him to enjoy himself without being so Royal and always surrounded by equerries and obsequious courtiers.

Of course wherever he went, if it became known, there would be a large crowd of people gathered to catch a glimpse of him.

'For tonight at any rate,' Wenda told herself, 'only the people in this house know he is here.'

Robbie had put all the gentlemen on the opposite side of the corridor and without saying anything to Wenda, he had put the ladies of their choice as nearly opposite each of them as possible. Therefore they only had to cross the corridor.

He had been on their parties before and he knew that the gentlemen taking part waited until everything was quiet before venturing out of their own room.

*

That certainly applied to the Marquis of Mildenhall.

He never hurried himself if he could help it.

At twenty-nine he had remained unmarried despite every effort on the part of his relatives to force him to take a wife.

As had been pointed out to him a thousand times he owned one of the finest houses in England with an estate that gave him better shooting than even Sandringham.

He also possessed a large and impressive house in London and he was one of the fortunate owners of a house designed by Nash in Regents Park.

"What are you waiting for?" his grandmother had asked him for the hundredth time only a week ago.

"I might seem a little old-fashioned these days," the Marquis replied, "but I am waiting to fall in love."

"Good Heavens, Victor, you must have done that a dozen times already!" the Dowager exclaimed.

The Marquis had smiled before he countered,

"Not exactly to my satisfaction."

"If you get much older, they will be saying you are too old to marry a young girl. Then you will be left with those improper married women I disapprove of."

She spoke with a particular lilt in her voice and a light in her eyes that told him she understood that he much preferred to 'play the field'.

"All I want," she said, "is for you to have an heir, perhaps two or three sons to carry on the name. And to appreciate the Mildenhall horses that in your grandfather's day won every classic race."

The Marquis had laughed.

"It is what I intend to do myself, Grandmama, and you must say I have been quite successful so far."

"So far is not good enough. Perhaps a bride would make you more ambitious and more determined to win."

He had laughed again.

Yet he had thought tonight, as he saw Robbie and Josofine together, that he was missing something.

'Why do I never feel like that?' he asked himself.

Then he looked at the lady sitting next to him and she was certainly extremely attractive. She was witty and amusing and had a complacent husband who spent a great deal of his time fishing and so he was not annoyed when his wife was a guest at one of the Prince of Wales's secret parties.

But the Marquis was honest with himself.

He realised that her attraction for him was not as strong as it might have been and it was only a question of time before he drifted away and looked for someone else.

'I wonder why,' he quizzed, 'that once I have tasted the forbidden fruit I find myself no longer interested in it.'

And he supposed the same could be said of all the gentlemen sitting round the table.

The Prince of Wales found it quite impossible to be faithful to any woman for long and then he was invariably searching for someone new.

Then once again the Marquis saw the happiness in Josofine's lovely face and what amounted to adoration in Robbie's.

'Why can I not feel like that?' he asked himself again.

He supposed dismally it was something that would never happen to him.

Of course he enjoyed making love to the beautiful ladies who went willingly into his arms as soon as he held them out, but at the same time he knew that it was not a very difficult victory and sooner than he really wanted he would be looking elsewhere for someone to take her place.

"The trouble with you, my dear Victor," one of his discarded mistresses had scoffed at him, "is that you are far too conceited and too pleased with yourself to give any woman your heart."

She had said it angrily rather than reproachfully and he found himself wondering if it was true.

Then he told himself that no man could control his own heart and if it did not respond in the way he wished it to do, that was not his fault.

The lady in question had not the facility or perhaps the magical attraction Robbie found in Josephine.

'They are making me feel much older,' the Marquis thought as he saw them disappearing when the Prince of Wales led the way up the stairs.

The room which had been allotted to him was very attractive and the Marquis walked across to the window that overlooked the garden.

It was then, as he pulled back the curtain a fraction, he saw Robbie and Josofine.

They were walking hand in hand past the fountain and then they disappeared into the trees and bushes at the other end of the lawn.

For a moment the Marquis wondered where they were going and then he could just see the roof of a Wendy House peeping through the leaves.

Quite suddenly the Marquis knew it was something he would like to be doing himself.

They were to be married, as the Prince of Wales had told everyone at dinner when they drank their health and Robbie had only to wait until Sunday before he made Josofine his.

Again the Marquis knew he was envious of them.

He too wanted to feel their inexpressible delight in being near each other and in love.

'That is exactly what I want and what I have been searching for,' he mumbled to himself.

Because it upset him to know he had failed so far, he pulled back the curtains sharply and started to undress.

The four-poster bed looked most inviting and he almost wished that Lady Eleanor, who he had brought with him, was not waiting on the other side of the corridor.

Then he told himself he was being ridiculous.

He had always enjoyed these secret parties of the Prince of Wales and of course he was enjoying this one.

Yet almost involuntarily he took longer with his undressing and washing, although he had had a bath before dinner and then he tidied his hair in front of the mirror.

With a little sigh that left his lips before he could control it, he opened the door.

He knew that as usual the ladies would have their names on the doors opposite.

Then he was aware that two of the candles which lit the corridor in silver sconces had gone out.

He had thought the corridor slightly dark when they had all come to bed, and yet he knew Lady Eleanor's room would be opposite to his, so it would not matter if he was unable to read her name on the card on her door.

Because he had taken a long time looking out of the window and undressing, the corridor was quiet.

He crossed it quickly and opened the door.

As he went into the room he thought he must be dreaming or else staring at one of the pictures he had seen on every wall and which he knew were all superb.

Looking across the room he could see lying in a four-poster – an *angel*.

She was breathtakingly beautiful, that went without saying. Her very fair hair fell in waves on either side of her face onto her shoulders.

There was a halo behind her head and the Marquis thought he would have known she was an *angel* without it.

At the age of fifteen Wenda had come down from the schoolroom and she had then slept on the same corridor as her father and mother.

Her mother had arranged Wenda's bedroom in a way she knew would please her. The four-poster instead of being heavy as so many of them were was light.

There were butterflies and tiny birds decorating the posts and at the end of the bed Lady Creswell had arranged curtains of muslin and lace for her daughter.

Because she knew it would please Wenda, she had put embroidered golden stars on the back of the bed behind the pillows – the centre one was large and directly behind her head as she sat propped up against her pillows.

As it caught the light from the candles it looked to the Marquis standing just inside the door like a halo.

For a moment he could only stand starring at what to him was a supernatural vision.

Then, aware that the door was open, Wenda asked in a low voice,

"Is that you, Robbie?"

The Marquis walked forward and reached the bed.

Wenda looked up in surprise.

"I thought you were Robbie."

"He is out in the garden," the Marquis answered.

Looking at him Wenda thought, as she had when she had seen him at dinner, he was a very handsome man – tall with wide shoulders, a square forehead and dark hair, he was better looking than any other man at the table.

Now because he just stood staring at her, she said,

"Your room is on the other side of the passage."

The Marquis was very quick-witted.

He realised instantly, although it surprised him, that she had no idea that he would have left his room for some particular reason.

Playing the part expected of him, he replied,

"I left something downstairs and went to fetch it. Actually the candles next to this door have gone out."

"Oh dear!" Wenda exclaimed. "I was afraid they were rather small and insignificant, but they were all we could find in such a hurry."

"Who are you?" the Marquis asked her. "Do you live here?"

With a jerk Wenda remembered what Robbie had said – on no account was anyone to know she was here in the house or that she was his sister.

There was a short hesitation before she replied,

"I am helping out with the cooking and I hope you enjoyed the French dishes at dinner."

The Marquis smiled.

"They were delicious, but I thought when I came into the room that you were not an inhabitant of this planet but – an *angel*."

Wenda gave a little laugh and he thought it was the most attractive sound he had ever heard.

"I wish I was," she answered him. "It would be so lovely to fly up to the sky and not to have to worry about all the problems down here on earth."

"I think that is something we all do occasionally, but if I come here in the morning, I am sure I will find this an empty room except for dust and mice."

Wenda laughed again, although she thought Robbie would be angry at her for talking to one of the guests.

"I think you ought to go to bed," she suggested. "You will find your room opposite this one and just a little to the left."

"Are you sending me away?" the Marquis asked. "I always thought *angels* were soft and gentle and willing to help those who needed it."

"I don't believe you need help," Wenda replied, "and although I don't know you, I am sure your horses are as magnificent as those that arrived here this afternoon. I am only hoping they will not find the new jumps we have installed either too high or too low."

The Marquis smiled.

"I feel sure they will be perfect like everything else in this house. I have never seen such magnificent pictures, nor eaten a better dinner nor met an *angel* before!"

"By the morning I will be gone," Wenda told him. "But if there is anything you may desire, then of course, if I pray hard enough for you, you will receive it."

It flashed through the Marquis's mind that what he really wanted was to feel as happy as Robbie and Josofine were at this very moment.

Then very much to his surprise, Wenda who had been looking up at him, added,

"*You will find it*. I know instinctively what you want and you will find it. When you do, it will make you tremendously happy.

"Are you telling me you are reading my thoughts?"

There was a little pause before Wenda answered,

"Sometimes I know what people are thinking. But usually they are people I know and love and I suppose that makes it easier."

"So you know," the Marquis said slowly, "that I was wishing for love."

"I realise that it is in your mind and of course it is something we all wish for. I know almost as if a voice is telling me that you *will* find love.

"It will be when your heart meets someone else's heart who is looking for you as you are looking for her."

Wenda spoke very softly and the Marquis listened to her almost as if he was hypnotised.

Then there was a strange silence between them.

They just gazed at each other.

At last the Marquis sighed,

"I just don't believe you are real. I am terrified that tomorrow I will not be able to find you again."

Wenda smiled.

"I think you should go to bed and please don't tell anyone, especially Robbie, that you found me here."

"I promise you I will do as you ask," the Marquis replied. "At the same time I do so want to see you again."

"That is impossible and please now go away. You should not have come here and, as I told you, your room is on the other side of the passage."

For a moment the Marquis thought he would defy her and then he complied,

"I will do what you tell me. But I swear if you are really a human being and not an illusion come from the sky above, I will find you again."

Although she did not reply, she was still looking up at him and the halo was shining behind her fair hair.

"Pray for me, my *angel*," the Marquis muttered.

He moved towards the door and when he reached it, he looked back.

Wenda was sitting as he had first seen her with the halo glinting in the candlelight behind her head.

As he walked into the corridor he knew that tonight at any rate he would not visit Lady Eleanor.

He went into his room and then he did something he had never done before on this sort of occasion.

He locked his door.

*

When he had gone, Wenda gave a sigh of relief.

She had felt half-afraid all the time he was standing there that Robbie would suddenly come in to tell her what was happening.

The Marquis had said that he had seen him in the garden and she had no idea if it was just to look at the fountain or if they had gone to the Wendy House. She had a feeling now that was what they had done.

Equally she knew Robbie would have been angry if he had found her talking to the Marquis.

She was supposed not to exist.

But it had been very exciting seeing him close to.

There had been a sincere note in his voice and it had told her that, although he had made strange remarks, he had not been laughing at her.

'I like him and I would love to talk to him again,' Wenda mused.

But she knew that was impossible.

She must just forget he had come into her room by mistake. It was because the candles in the sconce outside her door had gone out.

It had been difficult to buy so many candles in such a short time and she had had to rely on the village shop. And as she might have expected, they did not have enough candles to fill all the sconces.

She was also afraid of spending too much money and she had therefore told Mr. Twillet who kept the shop to procure her the cheapest he could find. They had been rather thin and were obviously foreign, but she had been thankful to have them without having to pay more.

Now she thought it might have been a case of being 'penny wise and pound foolish'.

She blew out the candles by her bed and snuggled down on the pillows.

'He is very handsome,' she told herself, 'and I have never talked to a man in that way before – '

But then she had talked with very few men.

She went to sleep and to her surprise dreamt of the Marquis asking her to pray for him.

*

When she awoke she looked at the clock and found it was still very early although it was already light.

It was then she had a sudden idea which had never occurred to her before.

She had been so busy in the house and working on the pictures and had therefore not had time to look at the Racecourse with its new jumps – Mr. Wentworth had only told her what he had done.

'If I get up now,' she surmised, 'I will be able to ride round the Racecourse. I might even take Samson over one or two of the jumps.'

Samson was the one fine stallion that remained of her father's horses that had always been outstanding. He had been still very young and more or less untrained when her father died. But he was well-bred and she had broken him in herself.

Now she realised that Samson must be wondering what had happened.

She had not ridden him since Robbie had presented her with such an appalling task.

But she had done it.

She had made the house habitable for the Prince of Wales.

Hurriedly she climbed out of bed and putting on her riding skirt and a white muslin blouse, she tied back her hair with a blue ribbon.

Without worrying any further about her looks, she ran down the stairs.

It was still far too early for even the most ardent servant to be working.

Only as she passed the kitchen did she hear Mr. and Mrs. Banks talking to each other and she guessed that like herself they would be too excited to sleep for long and they were now up before anyone else preparing breakfast.

Even if she was a little late it would not matter as Mrs. Banks not only had her assistance but there were two women from the village. They were both good cooks in their own way and had been assigned to the kitchen.

It had been Banks's suggestion and Wenda had not argued with him, knowing that he was thinking not of her but of his wife and he knew that if they gave her too much to do she might collapse and then be unable to do anything.

Without seeing anyone, Wenda went into the stable yard and when she opened the larger stable she was thrilled to see a dozen magnificent horses.

They belonged to the visitors and she had been told they were arriving yesterday, but she had been far too busy to go and see them.

Now she went to Samson's stall and even though he was not as well-bred as the new arrivals, he was still an outstanding stallion, one any man would be proud to own.

Samson was delighted to see Wenda and nuzzled against her affectionately.

She put on his saddle and bridle, suspecting that Ben and the newcomers' grooms were still asleep – they had been allocated rooms above the stables.

Now, as she rode out of the stable yard, she felt for the moment free of any further worries and cares.

"Let's enjoy ourselves, Samson," she cried, "and if these new jumps are too high for you, they will be too high for the visiting horses."

She always talked to Samson and he twitched his ears as if he understood.

When they reached the Racecourse she realised that Mr. Wentworth had done a very good job. There might be a certain roughness about the jumps, but they were firmly in place and the Racecourse really looked inviting.

As if Samson knew without being told what was expected of him, he took the first jump without hesitation.

They carried on to the next jump and then the next and Wenda thought it was all so exhilarating.

She had no idea that she was being watched.

*

The Marquis had had a sleepless night.

He had given up trying not to think of the *angel* he had encountered so unexpectedly.

He had therefore risen even earlier than Wenda.

His own house was a very large one and it was built to more or less the same design as Creswell Court.

He had thus easily found his way out of the back door and along the path that led to the stables where he found his stallion.

He had sent him down earlier, as the other visitors had sent theirs, because the Prince of Wales had told him there was a Racecourse at The Court.

Mountebank was indeed a fine animal with Arab blood in him and the Marquis was determined, if they raced as His Royal Highness intended, that he would be the winner.

He did not saddle Mountebank himself. He woke a rough-looking boy who was sleeping on a bale of hay.

He rubbed his eyes when he was told to get up and saddle the horse.

"It may seem too early for you," the Marquis said, "but I want to have a ride and it's a nice morning."

The boy did not answer and the Marquis found that he had to locate his saddle and bridle himself and watch that the girths were right and the bridle properly adjusted.

He only hoped that later in the day there would be better and more experienced grooms, but he admitted that it was his own fault for rising so early.

'There will surely be no one else out riding at this ridiculous hour,' he told himself.

Then without bothering to ask the boy he rode out of the stables to where he felt the paddock must be and it was not difficult from there to view the Racecourse.

To his astonishment he saw that he was not the only rider at this early hour.

Someone else was there already.

And to his amazement as he drew a little nearer he saw that it was a woman.

The rising sun shining on her fair hair without a hat made him think that once again he had found his *angel*.

Then he told himself he was just being absurd.

Was it likely that a young girl, looking as if she had just come down from the sky, would be out riding?

What was more she was jumping in a superb and almost professional fashion and watching her the Marquis thought she was undoubtedly the best female rider he had ever seen.

The way she was methodically taking one jump after another was astounding.

As he waited she turned round at the end of the course and came towards him.

There were two more very high jumps before she reached him and her mount took them magnificently, each one with six inches to spare.

It was when she took the last jump that the horse stumbled a little on landing because the ground was rough and the Marquis thought she might fall.

But with a superb piece of riding she managed to keep her horse on its feet and not to fall off herself.

For a moment the Marquis had held his breath.

Then as Wenda rode towards him he realised he had not been mistaken. It was the *angel* he had seen last night who had said she would pray for him.

Wenda was bending forward to pat Samson and she was telling him he was not to worry or be upset at almost tumbling over.

"You were splendid," she said in her soft voice, "as you always are. And you are far better than all the other horses put together."

She was looking down at Samson as she spoke and then as she looked ahead she saw the Marquis.

He had been standing with a tree behind him so that she had not noticed him until now.

As she drew up beside him, he exclaimed,

"How is it possible you can ride like that? Every jump here is far too high for a woman."

Wenda chuckled.

"I am not jumping them, Samson is. He says they are just the right height for him and he is quite certain if there is to be a race today he will win it."

She spoke in a way that made him laugh too.

"You are very confident," he smiled. "But I believe you are using supernatural powers to make sure of being the winner and that naturally is cheating!"

"Unfortunately I will not be riding," replied Wenda.

"Why not?" the Marquis asked.

"Because, as I have told you, I will be very busy in the kitchen."

"I don't believe you. No one could look like you and be nothing but a cook."

"You did admit last night that I was a very good cook. If you have had second thoughts, I will be very hurt and disappointed."

"I am not criticising the food. I am only saying it is impossible for anyone who looks like you to ride so well. At the same time to look, as you did last night, as if you might just float away on the first puff of wind blowing in through the window."

"That is such a lovely idea and I wish it was true, so perhaps that is what I should do!"

"I forbid you to do anything of the sort. Now tell me the truth about yourself, because I want to know."

"Think how disappointing it will be if you solve the problem, if there is one," Wenda countered, "without really making an effort."

She was silent for a moment and as the Marquis did not speak, she went on,

"I often think that life would be very dull if one was not often faced with problems of some sort."

She gave a sigh.

"Sometimes they are almost too overwhelming and challenging."

"It was very exciting for me last night," replied the Marquis, "to find you so unexpectedly."

"But you did promise me that you would not tell anyone you had found me."

"I never break my promise."

"That is what I want to hear."

Wenda tightened her reins and was just about to ride off when the Marquis called out,

"Where are you going and why are you leaving me?"

"You know I am not supposed to meet you. If you are up, there may be others in the party who think they will take a ride before breakfast."

"It is still very early," persisted the Marquis, "and I so want to talk to you."

It occurred to Wenda that she wanted to talk to him as well and it would be very intriguing for her to do so.

But she was afraid of upsetting Robbie.

"I have to go back," she told him, "and please just forget you have ever seen me. I know that Samson will not talk and no one must know he has just taken all the jumps without any effort."

"You can trust me," the Marquis promised. "But you must sense that I have to see you again."

"It will be just impossible, but I am still praying you will find what you are seeking."

As she said the last words she rode away before the Marquis could stop her.

He felt if he hurried after her into the stable yard it might be embarrassing, so he then took Mountebank over the jumps all the time thinking about Wenda.

How could he find out exactly who she was without breaking his promise?

And why was he not to speak about her to Robbie?

He knew without being told there were no sinister reasons for this.

If she had been an ordinary woman, he would have thought she was perhaps one of Robbie's lovers, someone he did not think grand enough to meet the Prince of Wales.

But there was a purity and an innocence about his *angel* which told him that she had never been kissed.

The Marquis was still thinking about Wenda when later he went in to breakfast to find that most of the guests, including the Prince of Wales, were already downstairs.

"I hear you have been riding already, Victor," the Prince called out to him.

"Creswell has an excellent course of jumps, sir, and I am determined that my horse should win today!"

There were protests at this from the others.

As Robbie came in he apologised for being late and the Prince of Wales enquired,

"Tell me about your Racecourse, Robbie. Victor has set his heart on winning today. He has already jumped the gun by exploring it while we were asleep in bed."

"I am prepared to say that is cheating, sir. But his horses are always so good that he will doubtless beat us all anyway even if he is handicapped."

"Now you are being a bit aggressive," the Marquis protested, "and if you are riding a magnificent horse called Samson, which I saw in the stable this morning, I think *you* will have an unfair advantage."

They were laughing at each other, but the Marquis was well aware that Robbie had no idea that Samson had already been round the jumps.

He had already admitted they had been erected very quickly simply because the old course was in such a bad state of repair.

The Marquis recalled how Samson had stumbled at the last fence and suggested,

"I thought this morning there is one place which is dangerous and which should be attended to before we start any racing."

Robbie asked him exactly where it was and when the Marquis explained, he responded,

"I will see to it immediately, although I am sure you will think the man who put up the fences has done a good job."

"An excellent one," the Marquis agreed.

He wondered as he spoke whether the *angel* had in some way arranged this as well as the cooking and then he told himself that he must most definitely learn the truth about her before he was obliged to leave Creswell Court.

When Robbie left the breakfast table he managed to catch Banks before he entered the room.

"Please tell Miss Wenda to meet me immediately in the Estate Office."

Banks nodded and hurried to the kitchen.

Five minutes later when Robbie had gone into the Estate Office, Wenda joined him.

"I went to your room," he said, "but you were not there. I imagine you were in the kitchen."

"Yes, of course, Robbie," Wenda answered him.

She had changed from her riding habit as soon as she returned to the house, and she was now wearing an old dress from which the colour had been washed out and an overall that belonged to Mrs. Banks.

"Dinner was superb last night," Robbie praised her, "but what I really want to tell you about is myself."

"I saw the Prince of Wales drinking a health last night and I thought it was for you but I could not hear what he was saying."

"I suspected you were in the minstrels' gallery. I thought that you would go there."

"I wanted to have a look at you all. It was really fantastic and rather like something on the stage. I felt it could not be happening in real life and in our house!"

"But it was, Wenda, and now I have a great deal to tell you, but we don't have much time."

He told her the story of how he had met Josofine.

And how he had fallen in love with her, but had not known who she was until she had arrived at The Court and how the Prince of Wales had recognised her.

"So you must understand," he finished, "that she is not Madame Frazer, which actually was the name of her mother. She is in fact La Comtesse de Mouchy and we are to be married tomorrow immediately after luncheon before His Royal Highness drives back to London."

"*Tomorrow*!" exclaimed Wenda.

"It is what I have planned and the Vicar is coming to see us in the morning."

For a moment Wenda could only stare at him.

"I had never expected you to get married, Robbie, because we have so little money."

"Marriages in France are arranged and in fact she is very rich. To run away was the only way Josofine could escape becoming the wife of the man she hates."

"I think it was very brave of her."

"Of course it was," Robbie agreed, "and when you get to know her you will love her as I do. She is indeed a wonderful, wonderful girl and I am the luckiest man in the whole world."

"If she is an heiress," Wenda asked him cautiously, "you will be able to live here?"

"She has already said that is what she wants to do and we intend to make the house even grander."

Robbie was smiling as he added,

"Oh, Wenda, is this really happening? I am so afraid I will wake up and discover that it is all part of my imagination."

"I think Papa and Mama will be delighted that you will still be able to live here at The Court and in the way they did when they were first married."

"It's all too incredible," Robbie cried. "I know you will love Josofine as soon as you meet her."

There was silence then Wenda murmured,

"I *must* come to your wedding."

"Of course you must, Wenda, and you must come as yourself. The only thing you can do, and I have thought it out very carefully, is to arrive at the Church and pretend you have been staying with relatives or friends nearby."

Wenda stared at him.

"As you are engaged, why cannot I arrive tonight?"

Robbie wondered if he should tell her the truth and then he thought it would be a mistake.

"I think it might upset the Prince, who only likes his own friends at these special house parties. It would also put the numbers out and we should be a man short."

"Yes, of course I see," agreed Wenda, "I will arrive at the Church tomorrow at two o'clock and no one will know I have just cooked the luncheon!"

Robbie laughed.

"You have been absolutely marvellous, my dearest sister. It is all due to you that everything has gone so well and His Royal Highness is in the best temper I have ever known."

"Well, keep him like that," replied Wenda, "and I do naturally want to meet him."

"What I want you to do and it might be rather a rush, is to get Mrs. Banks and the people in the kitchen to help you make us a wedding cake. I know Josofine will not feel married unless we have one. So please, Wenda, make one. It need not be very large as there will be no one coming to the wedding except the house party."

"I would not like to bet on it, Robbie, and I suppose you realise that once the village knows you are married, they will expect fireworks and barrels of beer on the lawn as when you celebrated your twenty-first birthday."

"I remember that and of course you are right. You must promise them it is exactly what they will have when I return from my honeymoon."

"Have you decided where you are going, Robbie?"

"We have been discussing it, but the great problem is if I meet her father and mother, the Duc and Duchesse, before we go on our honeymoon or after we come back."

"I will give you the answer to that. Enjoy yourself while you can and give them a chance to recover from the shock."

"You are a genius, Wenda. Why did I not think of that, but Josofine does not want to make them any angrier than they are already, after all she is turning down a ruling Prince to marry just me."

"I think it is very very sensible of her. You are an exceptional person and you should be very grateful to His Royal Highness as he will make everything plain sailing for you. And if he is blessing your marriage, the Duc will not dare to go against him."

"You are absolutely right and I did actually think of that myself," Robbie exclaimed.

He kissed her and sighed,

"When we come back, I am going to insist on your having a grand ball in London. You will undoubtedly be the belle of the Season and no one will equal you."

"I look forward to that, Robbie, and I am crossing my fingers in case it does not happen."

Robbie laughed and then he hurried away because he knew the Prince of Wales would soon be ready to go to the Racecourse.

Wenda went into the kitchen and told Mrs. Banks and the other women what they had to do.

Because they were so delighted at the idea, they all agreed that his Lordship must have a magnificent cake and they only hoped there would be enough time to decorate it.

"I've got an idea," said Mrs. Banks. "Although you may think it's wrong, it's the best thing us can do quickly."

"What is that?" Wenda asked her.

"I remembers that the cake we had for your mother and father's Silver Wedding were a very big one. They asks everyone in the County here and even some from the village like the doctor and the Vicar and his wife."

Because Mrs. Banks was always a bit long-winded, Wenda listened and tried not to look impatient.

"What we had on that occasion were a huge three-tiered cake. It be so well decorated that us only made the top two layers and the bottom was all pretty with flowers and little emblems so it were not eaten so to speak."

"You mean it was false," enquired Wenda.

"Yes, that's the word," Mrs. Banks replied. "And us had slices of a separate cake on the side which us hand round and they has no idea it didn't come off the pretty one."

"For this wedding we will be very few so we could decorate the lower layers and just make the top one real."

"That be what I were thinking, Miss Wenda."

Mrs. Banks paused for breath before she added,

"It'll save us a lot of trouble and I'm certain that with your paintbrush you'd soon touch up the old bits and make them look like new."

"We will certainly give it a try and someone can tell Mrs. Stevenson that we want to look for it in the attic."

"She be up there already," one of the women came in. "The young lady that his Lordship's to marry needs a weddin' dress badly and she's got a whole lot of 'em – your mother's dress, your grandmother's and your great-grandmother's. She's talked about 'em often enough."

Wenda could not wait to find Mrs. Stevenson and ask her if she had told Robbie about the wedding gowns.

"Of course he knows about them," the housekeeper replied. "The gowns are on the lady's bed and she's going into ecstasies over them."

"Do you think she'll wear Mama's?" asked Wenda.

"As she is small and so was your grandmother, I think then it'll be either your grandmother's or your great-grandmother's with the lovely veil they both wore and the brides before them too."

Wenda thought it all very thrilling and she wished she could see the gowns and help Josofine, but she knew that she must not interfere.

And Robbie would be angry with her for appearing before she was supposed to do so.

When she was in her own room later in the evening, she wished she had a smart dress she could wear herself as all her clothes looked drab and dull.

While the wedding gowns had been preserved over the years, unfortunately all the other dresses, as they had fallen out of fashion, had been given away or destroyed.

It was when the men were changing for dinner that she waited in her bedroom.

She knew she should have been in the kitchen, but she was sure that Robbie would come to her, as she had left a note on his dressing table to say she must see him.

When she could hear several of the guests talking as they came up the stairs, she knew he would not be long.

He opened the door of her room and when he came in, he could see that she was looking worried.

"What has happened, Wenda?" he asked.

"I don't have a dress fit to wear tomorrow and they have all told me what lovely clothes your Josofine has. I wonder if she would be kind enough to lend me a dress just to appear in the Church – "

For a moment he stared at her and then he said,

"You must think I am treating you very badly in not introducing you to the House Party. It would be a mistake to involve the Prince of Wales, but there is no reason why you should not meet Josofine and she can be told what you have done for me. Stay here!"

He ran from the room.

Two minutes later he came back with Josofine.

She was wearing a dressing gown and was saying,

"What has happened? Where are you taking me?"

Robbie pulled her into the room and shut the door.

"I want you to meet someone who is responsible for everything that has happened here. For the cooking, the cleaning of the house, for the jumps on the Racecourse and the reason we will be fortunate enough to have a really lovely wedding tomorrow."

Josofine looked bewildered.

"If dearest Wenda – my sister – had not organised everything," Robbie went on, "I would have had to refuse His Royal Highness's suggestion of coming here to stay and you would never have met him with me."

"Your sister," Josofine exclaimed. "But why have I not met her before?"

"Because she has been in the background making everything possible, but I will tell you all about it another time."

He knew that, just like Wenda, Josofine had no idea why the Prince of Wales had these secret parties to which every man brought the lady of his choice.

"Well, I am delighted to have a sister," Josofine sighed as Robbie stopped talking.

"That is a very nice thing to say," added Wenda, "and I am so glad you and Robbie are so happy."

"It is the most wondrous unbelievable thing that has ever happened to me," Josofine replied. "He is so kind, and I was so terrified he would not fall in love with me."

"It was not difficult," Robbie smiled.

Just for a moment they looked at each other and forgot that Wenda was there.

Then Josofine said,

"Robbie tells me that you want something to wear at our wedding and you must have anything you want. We are going to Paris later, where I can buy clothes in which I will really look beautiful for him. Otherwise he might be disappointed in me."

"That is impossible," sighed Robbie.

She gave him a flashing smile before she turned to Wenda,

"Come to my room – "

"No!" interrupted Robbie, "that would be a mistake in case anyone realises Wenda is here. And if she does not help in the kitchen with the French dishes for dinner, His Royal Highness may be in a disagreeable mood and refuse to give you away."

Josofine gave a cry of horror.

"I tell you what I will do now, Wenda. When I go downstairs I will put all of my clothes at your disposal. Looking at you I think you will look prettiest in pink or perhaps in a very soft blue."

"You don't mind if I wear it for the wedding?"

"When I come back from Paris," Josofine replied, "as we are more or less the same size I will bring you some fashionable dresses as a present."

She looked at Robbie as she spoke and as he could not find any words, he kissed her hand.

"You are so kind and I am hugely happy for you," said Wenda. "I promise you your cake is going to be very impressive, but I don't want to be an encumbrance to you."

"You could never be that," Robbie added firmly. "I am going to tell Josofine about the ball I will give for you after we are married and buy a decent house in London where we can entertain."

"I don't believe what I am hearing," Wenda cried. "It is too wonderful and I just know you will both be happy here."

"Of course we will. We would be happy anywhere, but Josofine will be the most beautiful chatelaine who has ever reigned in Creswell Court."

"That is a lovely compliment," Josofine sighed and kissed Robbie's cheek.

Then she kissed Wenda.

"You will be needing a hat as well as a dress and they will all be waiting for you when I go downstairs."

"Thank you, thank you," enthused Wenda, "and I am so thrilled for you both I feel I want to cry."

"Don't do that," Robbie replied. "If you do I will find this is a dream and will wake up. It was what I felt when I first met Josofine and I still feel it cannot be real."

"It is! It is!" cried Josofine, "and now, whatever Papa may feel, I cannot be made to marry that horrible German Prince."

"I will kill anyone who tries to take you from me," Robbie answered stubbornly. "At the same time we will both be in disgrace if we are late for dinner!"

Josofine gave a little cry, kissed Wenda again and rushed out of the room.

"She is so delightful," Wenda murmured as Robbie turned towards the door. "You are very very lucky."

"I know and thank you again, dearest Wenda."

Robbie kissed his sister and then he too was gone.

Wenda hurried downstairs to put the last touches to the French dishes to be served at dinner and as she went she was thinking how wonderful it was for Robbie.

Then as she reached the kitchen she found herself thinking of herself.

She wondered if, once the wedding was over, she would ever see the Marquis again.

*

CHAPTER SEVEN

Wenda dressed herself in the beautiful blue dress she had chosen from those Josofine had left for her and the small hat trimmed with blue feathers to match was most becoming.

She knew when she had put them on she had never owned anything so expensive and all in such perfect taste.

She thought that her new sister-in-law would be an extremely nice person to live with.

Then as she thought of it she gave a sudden start.

Where would she go?

What would she do?

They had not said a word so far about her staying on at The Court.

But she knew quite clearly that whatever they said they would not really want her as of course when they were first married they would want to be alone together.

She could not live in the house without being with them.

'What shall I do? Where shall I go?' she agonised frantically.

She left her room and went down the backstairs as she must not be seen by the guests who she reckoned were now congregating in the front hall.

Carriages were carrying them to the Church which was only at the end of the drive.

Josofine would leave last with the Prince of Wales, who had thrown himself wholeheartedly into organising the wedding.

He had told the Vicar exactly what he required and Robbie, who had been listening, knew he was delighted to be taking orders from someone so distinguished.

"I do hope Your Royal Highness understands," the Vicar said, "that, although I will try to keep this wedding as secret as possible, I suspect that the village is already aware that Your Royal Highness is here at Creswell Court, and they will undoubtedly find their way into the Church."

The Prince of Wales laughed.

"Let them," he asserted. "Everyone always enjoys a wedding and it is only fair that this young couple should share their happiness with others."

As he listened, Robbie knew that, as he had said himself, he was the luckiest man in the world.

Not only was he marrying the one woman he really loved and that she loved him, but all their difficulties were being ironed out by the Prince of Wales.

As Wenda was to learn later from Mrs. Stevenson, the gown which had been worn by their grandmother when she was married fitted Josofine perfectly.

As it was the time when the fashion had been for very full skirts, it had a natural train at the back and she would look lovely with the large Creswell tiara holding in place the glorious Brussels lace veil that had been used by Cresswell brides for three centuries.

Robbie had gone to Wenda's room early in the morning while she was still in bed.

She had deliberately not gone out riding as she had done the morning before as she thought, if the Marquis was riding too, they might be seen and it would annoy her brother.

He had to knock loudly on her door because when he turned the handle he found to his surprise it was locked.

When she let him in Robbie asked,

"Why did you lock your door? I have never known you to do so before."

"I thought someone might come in by mistake and see me," answered Wenda.

She had actually locked the door because she was afraid that, just as he had come in by mistake last night and called her an *angel*, the Marquis would come to speak to her again.

She wanted to see him, she wanted it fervently, but she knew it would be wrong.

He might guess who she was or ask Robbie if she really was working in the kitchen. In which case Robbie would be very angry with her.

Also at the back of her mind she knew her mother would be shocked at the idea of anyone coming into her bedroom while she was in bed.

It had been such a difficult decision to make and one which she felt almost tore her in half.

'When he leaves today after the wedding, I will not see him again,' she thought. 'And if he did come to talk to me once again, as he did last night, it would be something to remember.'

Then she realised it was selfish to think of herself rather than Robbie and his instructions.

"You must see to the wedding cake and everything else in the dining room, Wenda," he insisted. "Then come out through the back door and reach the Church before the house party and well before the bride and the Prince of Wales arrive."

"Am I to walk?" Wenda asked him.

She thought in the smart dress Josofine had lent her she would attract the attention of those driving down from the front door.

"No, of course not," Robbie answered. "I am not as stupid as that, I have arranged for Ben to take you. I am afraid it is in the old carriage since we have nothing better. But at least you will arrive in style and he will take you back to The Court when the Service is over."

He paused before he added,

"Then you will be introduced to the house party who will be told you that have been staying with one of our relatives."

Wenda laughed.

"You really have thought it all out, Robbie."

"Just as you made the house as comfortable and as smart as it has been for the Prince of Wales, we will carry on your good work as soon as our honeymoon is over."

"You might tell me where you are going," Wenda suggested rather sulkily.

"Victor Mildenhall has kindly lent us his house at Newmarket. We are going to stay there and decide which racehorses we will buy as soon as we have finished doing up the house.

"Then when the Prince of Wales tells us we have been forgiven by Josofine's family, we will go to France to stay with the Duc and Duchesse and buy her trousseau."

"I feel rather uncomfortable at having taken one of her pretty dresses away," admitted Wenda.

"Just don't worry about it. She has already written a letter to the shop I took her to in Bond Street, telling them to send more clothes and I am quite certain trunkfuls of them will be coming to us in Newmarket!"

It was only when he had left that Wenda thought to herself how marvellous it must be to be so rich.

She had not asked Robbie for any more money, but just before he left her bedroom he had handed her a large envelope saying,

"Here is some money to pay the servants and the workmen. And do take out of it as much as you want for yourself."

She looked inside the envelope and gave a cry of astonishment.

"Two thousand pounds! Surely you cannot have drawn that from the bank."

"Josofine has made it possible. And I am not going to feel embarrassed about it. Of course we will have to spend her money in doing up the house exactly as we want it and to employ just as many servants as will make us comfortable. But it is *my* house, *my* estate and *my* pictures and I do have every intention of not being embarrassed by letting my wife contribute to our comfort!"

Wenda laughed and put her arms round his neck and kissed him.

"You are wonderful!" she exclaimed. "I know you will always be 'cock of the roost', and that is what every woman really likes her husband to be."

"I knew you would understand, Wenda."

Robbie kissed her and hurried away.

She thought again how lucky he was to have found someone so beautiful and at the same time so intelligent and understanding as Josofine.

The carriage was waiting at the kitchen door.

As she stepped in Mrs. Banks called out,

"Now don't you worry. I'll see that everything's perfect when you comes back, and you can be sure they'll be as pleased as punch when they sees that cake."

Wenda knew there was no doubt of their being anything else, as the cake now it was fully decorated with flowers and fruit, looked magnificent.

And so did the whole table.

As if it was not enough to make everything perfect for the Prince of Wales, the servants were now waiting for the bride and bridegroom.

Wenda was not at all surprised when she reached the Church to find that there was already a small crowd of villagers outside and a number had already sneaked in to sit in the pews at the very back.

She had been sure that, once the Prince of Wales had arrived at The Court, the women who were working in the house would inevitably tell their families and friends when they went home at night.

As she entered the Church the Vicar greeted her and walked with her to the family pew.

The house party, when they arrived, looked at her curiously.

Wenda was surprised at first not to see the Marquis and then when he did finally appear, he was walking beside Robbie and she realised he was to be his Best Man.

The Service was simple but very sincere.

Wenda prayed for her brother's happiness, but she felt that he had already been blessed by God in finding Josofine.

When the bride and bridegroom left, the house party followed them down the aisle to the carriages waiting for them outside.

Wenda's old carriage came last in the procession.

She had just climbed in when to her great surprise the Marquis, having helped some of the other guests into the first carriages, joined her.

As he got in beside her, he closed the door firmly and there was no question of their giving anyone else a lift.

"How could you have been so cruel," he asked her, "and so unkind as to shut me out of Paradise last night?"

Wenda blushed.

The Marquis thought it made her even lovelier than ever.

"I was afraid," Wenda answered him, "that Robbie might see you and he would have been angry with me."

"He told me before we left the house," the Marquis replied, "that his sister was arriving for the wedding after staying with relatives."

"Oh, please," Wenda pleaded, "you must be very careful not to let anyone know that I was in the house all the time."

"Were you really helping in the kitchen?"

"Of course I was. You don't suppose Mrs. Banks, good cook though she is, could have prepared those French dishes that I heard His Royal Highness enjoys so much."

"He certainly did. He took such large helpings I was afraid I was not going to get any!"

Wenda laughed.

"As soon as the bride and bridegroom have left," the Marquis said, "and of course His Royal Highness, I want to talk to you about *us*."

Wenda felt her heart give a little leap and it was with difficulty she managed to ask him,

"What do you mean by that?"

"I mean, Wenda, that I have just told Robbie I am looking after you, and I am taking you this afternoon, when everyone has gone and you are ready to leave, to stay with my grandmother."

"I cannot leave the house!" Wenda said quickly.

"From what I gather," he replied quietly, "your man Banks is perfectly capable of keeping the work going and you and I have to think of our future."

"I don't know – what you mean," Wenda answered him hesitatingly.

"I think you do, and as it is quite a long distance to my grandmother's, I suggest that when we arrive back now you instruct your housekeeper to pack your clothes."

There was no time to say anything more because the carriages had reached the house.

The bride and bridegroom had gone in and so had the Prince of Wales and most of the house party.

As Wenda got out she felt her head swimming.

It was impossible to think clearly what the Marquis meant or what was happening.

As soon as they reached the dining room, Robbie was at her side.

First he introduced her to the Prince of Wales.

"I have told you about my sister, sir," he began, "and how wonderful she has been in preparing everything for your visit."

"Then I must thank you very much," the Prince of Wales said as Wenda curtsied deeply to him. "I have never enjoyed a visit more or been more comfortable."

"That is exactly what I wanted to hear, Your Royal Highness."

"I am also delighted that your brother has acquired such a charming and pretty wife whom I have known ever since she was born," the Prince of Wales went on. "I look forward to entertaining them at Sandringham as soon as they return from their honeymoon."

Wenda felt this would go far to assuage the anger the Duc would be feeling at Josofine's refusal to marry the Prince he had chosen for her.

Everyone else in the house party was delighted to meet Wenda.

The Duchess of Manchester said to her,

"Please call on me when you come to London. I want to have a long talk about your pictures. Robbie tells me that you know more about them than anyone else."

"I have tried to remember everything my father told me about them and thank you so much for your invitation."

Whilst she was talking and being introduced, she was vividly conscious that the Marquis was watching her.

She still found it hard to believe that he was taking her away the moment everybody had departed.

After the Prince of Wales had sampled the wedding cake and proposed the health of the bride and bridegroom he was in a hurry to return to London.

As soon as he had left the rest of the party left too.

The Marquis had in some clever way arranged that Lady Eleanor should travel with the Duke of Sutherland and his lady friend in the Ducal carriage. Whether they were pleased or not, she went with them.

As the last of the guests drove away down the drive and Wenda was waving them all goodbye, she found the Marquis standing beside her.

"I have just told Banks," he said, "that I want my carriage brought round immediately so that we can set off as soon as you are ready."

Wenda looked up at him.

"Is this really happening?" she whispered. "I feel you are taking my breath away."

"That is just what I want to do, my *angel*."

Somehow because she was looking up into his eyes and he was looking into hers they said a great deal more than words.

Wenda realised that she must not keep him waiting and as she hurried up to her room a footman was already carrying her case down the stairs.

"I've put in all your best things, Miss Wenda," Mrs. Stevenson said, "and if you get the chance, you must buy yourself a new riding habit not to mention a dress or two."

She thought now with the large amount of money Robbie had given her she could spend a little on some new clothes. She felt uncomfortable at looking like a beggar-maid most of the time.

As if she had spoken aloud, Mrs. Stevenson said,

"I thinks your evening gown be a bit shabby, Miss Wenda, so I puts in some of your mother's dresses which are as fresh as the day she bought them. I've kept me eye on them and I thinks you'll find they won't look so out of fashion even now."

Wenda remembered that her mother had had one or two very pretty evening gowns which she had worn for the Hunt Ball and dinner parties. They had been put away and she had never thought of wearing them herself.

Indeed she had often felt as if her mother's clothes were too sacred to be worn by anyone else, but now she felt that they would be the blessing she badly needed.

"Thank you for organising it, Mrs. Stevenson. It is something I did not think of myself."

"You deserve a nice bit of fun, Miss Wenda, for all you've done. And now that things have changed for his Lordship this be a very happy house.

"His Lordship, before he left, said he couldn't do without me and I promised him I'd stay here and help her

Ladyship until she could manage The Court as well as you've always done."

"That is wonderful news!" exclaimed Wenda.

Just before she went downstairs Banks came up to see if the footmen had taken down everything she required.

"You have been marvellous, Banks," she said, "and His Royal Highness claimed he had never enjoyed himself more."

"That is just what his Lordship has told me and I understand that you're leaving us too, Miss Wenda."

"I am going to stay with a relative of the Marquis. I am not sure how long I shall be away, but I expect his Lordship told you that when you have spent all the money I am giving you now to pay the wages and buy food, you just have to be in touch with me."

She handed him an envelope in which there was a thousand pounds.

"Thank you, Miss Wenda. I'll pay all the workers weekly."

Then because she wanted to be with the Marquis she ran down the steps.

Outside drawn by four superb black horses was the smartest open carriage she had ever seen.

There was a seat behind for the groom, but when she got in she found that the turned-back cover completely obscured him. Nor would he be able to hear what she and the Marquis said to each other.

Banks waved them off.

As they trotted off down the drive with the Marquis driving, Wenda said a little nervously,

"Are you quite sure that your grandmother will be pleased to see me? After all you cannot have let her know that you are bringing me with you."

The Marquis waited until they had passed through the iron gates before he replied,

"My grandmother, Wenda, will welcome you with open arms. She has been begging me for years and years to get married, but I have always refused until now."

Wenda turned to look at him in sheer astonishment.

He looked back at her before he added,

"Surely you realise that you are what I have been searching for all my life but was certain did not exist!"

"I really – don't understand," Wenda whispered a little incoherently.

"I think you knew," said the Marquis, "when I first saw you and thought you were an *angel*, that having found you I would never lose you again."

"I never thought – of such a thing," Wenda tried to say.

"I realised next morning that we enjoyed the same pursuits and that you were so completely and absolutely the *angel* I was always told as a child looked after me and loved me."

Wenda drew in her breath.

Then, as the Marquis drove on down the road, she murmured in a voice he could only just hear,

"I thought – I would never see you again after the wedding."

"You are going to see me for the rest of my life," the Marquis replied, "and we are going to be married just as soon as you have met my family. Unlike your sister-in-law, I don't want you to start off on the wrong foot."

"I am sure that the Duc and Duchesse will forgive Josofine when they realise how happy Robbie and she are."

"They will forgive her because she was given away by the Prince of Wales," the Marquis added, "but they will always regret she is not a reigning Princess, however don't let's worry about them. I want you to think of me and only me."

"I have found it difficult to think of anything else," Wenda said, "ever since I first saw you from the minstrels' gallery."

The Marquis laughed.

"So you peeped at us from up there. I might have guessed that is what you would do. But I did not know until I went into your bedroom by mistake that an *angel* had come down from Heaven especially for me. Now my life will *never* be the same again."

"How can you be certain that when you know me better you will not be disappointed?" Wenda asked him.

"When I first saw you my heart turned a somersault and it has never gone back to its normal place. Every time I have seen you I have fallen more deeply in love than I have ever been in my whole life. I have never known a love like this, which I have read about and dreamt about, but which I believed would never happen to me."

"How can that be true," asked Wenda shyly, "when you are so handsome and so important."

"Is that why you love me?" the Marquis demanded.

"No, of course not," Wenda said without thinking.

Then she blushed again and looked away at the road ahead.

"So you *do* love me," he added quietly. "I thought you did, and when you locked your door last night, I was quite certain of it."

Wenda looked at him in surprise.

"Why do you say that?" she asked.

"Because if you were flirting with me, you would have left the door open and let me come to talk to you. But I think, my darling, you were afraid of yourself."

151

Wenda knew this to be true.

She wanted him, but she knew it was wrong for her to do so. She had been afraid of her own feelings.

There was no need for her to answer the Marquis.

As she looked towards him, he saw the expression in her eyes and exclaimed,

"You love me, I just know you love me and I can promise you, my dearest darling, we are going to be very very happy."

Wenda moved a little closer to him.

"I was thinking that when Robbie came back from his honeymoon with Josofine they would not want me at The Court and I wondered where I could go."

The Marquis did not answer and she went on,

"I wanted to be with you, but I never thought you would want me."

"I want you as I have never wanted any woman before, Wenda, and we are going to be married just as soon as my family has met you. Then I intend to teach you, my darling one, all about love – the love I have never known myself until now."

"It is so wonderful!" Wenda murmured, "that I am quite certain this is all a fantastic perfect dream."

"That is what it is going to be for the rest of our lives. My darling, there are so many things we are going to do together which I have been too lazy to do before, but which I will do now simply because I know that they will please you. We will enjoy making our part of the world, even if it is a small part, more perfect and an example to others."

He spoke very quietly and Wenda could not help moving a little closer to him.

"I love you, Victor" she whispered, "but I do know very little about love and you will have to teach me to love you in the way you want to be loved."

"You just have to be yourself. Don't forget you are an *angel* sent specially down from Heaven to me and that is how I first saw you sitting up in your bed. From that moment it has been impossible for me to think of anything else."

"I will try to be the *angel* you want me to be, but you will have to help me and teach me and of course go on loving me."

She spoke the last few words a little wistfully and he knew she was apprehensive.

"I will love you as long as I live," he declared, "and I believe when we die we will still be together just as we have been together before so often and have been searching for each other ever since."

"I am sure that is true," Wenda murmured.

As the Marquis drove the horses on, the sunshine seemed to envelope not only themselves but their hearts.

Wenda knew she had found something so perfect and so sublime that never again would she be afraid or lonely.

'Thank You God, thank You,' she prayed silently.

Then as the Marquis turned to look at her she knew that he was saying the same prayer as she was.